Here She Comes Now

S.J. McMahon

ACKNOWLEDGMENTS

I would like to thank my partner Jeff, all of my family and my friends for supporting my writing. Special thanks to Julie Frazer and Wayne Leeming for their editing skills.

CHAPTER 1

Euphoria, and an unusual sense of wellbeing.

He laughed. It was all so ridiculous. Seated in his car, in the dying light, his trousers unzipped, flesh on show, with someone who, it now appeared, wished to do him harm. But still, the euphoria. It was all that really mattered now.

After the initial shock of the assault, the strangeness of the needle piercing his arm, the tingling rush of the drug spreading through his veins, he realised he no longer cared about the situation he had found himself in, his disarray, or the motive of the person with him. He was simply drifting.

Never known anything like it, he thought, a lazy grin pulling at his face as he mused on this deeply comforting relaxed state.

The car rocked as the 'someone' exited. He rocked with it. The memory of a delicate lullaby stirred, and he was once more a tiny child being comforted by his mother. The inappropriateness of images of his mother at a time like this seemed darkly humorous, and bubbles of laughter gurgled in his throat.

The sound of the door slamming seemed to push deep and long into his mind. He watched the slender figure of his companion blur into the darkness.

Any interest in the world around him waned now. His only wish was to give in to this surprising new feeling, to go with it, sinking deeper into its warmth, allowing the world to diminish and darken.

CHAPTER 2

'Filthy beggars.'

Harry Wood poked the used condom from the bush into the black plastic bag.

'Not even my job. I'm security, not cleaning.'

The site manager was always lecturing the staff about making the place look like a professional business. So, Harry tried to do his bit. To keep a veneer of respectability over things.

Easier said than done on a business unit in the heart of the red-light district.

Harry knew the cleaners wouldn't touch the spoils of the late business dealings, much to the annoyance of the site manager and its owners.

To be fair, he understood the squeamishness of the cleaning staff. Plus, he didn't want anyone getting sacked over such a thing. So, it fell to him to 'mop up', so to speak.

The unit that Harry worked at was on a relatively modern industrial estate that had been crudely thrown up on the edge of the more historic part of the city. The wider area was expansive, with numerous redundant stone mill buildings. A tight network of narrow streets and alleys were darkened by looming stone industrial terraces of often richly ornate yet crumbling buildings.

The sturdy concrete legs of the motorway bypass created a natural cut-off to one side where more contemporary buildings had sprung up, including the estate Harry worked in. The rest of the area bled out into a more mixed cityscape.

Over the years, many of the more historic buildings had been randomly removed, like individual teeth knocked out by a punch to the mouth. In places, these had to be replaced by shiny new monoliths as modern commerce had attempted on occasions to nose its way into the area. Other patches had been left as piles of rubble that had long been retaken by nature.

The older businesses that had once dominated this patch had died when the textile industry had lost its prominence. The remaining majestic old structures had been taken over by newer enterprises, seeking cheap rents and the sort of privacy this place could offer.

The area had become known as the Triangle by straight-talking locals due to the shape of its mapped layout. Like its name-sake the Bermuda Triangle, it was easy to get lost down there.

Despite the area's free and easy approach to the less legal activities, the police did occasionally attempt to show some muscle. Random raids on the old mills would see officers staggering out with armfuls of skunk plants, or leading chains of downtrodden illegal workers.

However, when it came to the so-called oldest profession, the police and local council officials had agreed that, for an undefined temporary period, this would be informally decriminalized. So, the women and men who worked the Triangle plied their trade largely unhindered by the law. For the time being, at least.

Harry had worked 'the security' here from some 20 years and was sure that he must have seen it all. He was well aware that some of the young employees thought of him as some kind of relic from a long-gone era, but he consoled himself with the thought that it was nothing more than envy. Wasn't surprising really, he decided, him being such a senior member of staff, by experience and longevity, if not by his position in the pecking order.

He even had his own office these days. It was a converted storage cupboard in reality, but it was his domain. His own mini kingdom, he would joke to himself.

It made him feel respected though. Harry genuinely felt his long service gave him some sort of rank, plus a good dollop of knowledge and common sense that some of his younger colleagues, in his view, clearly did not possess. They certainly didn't know how to respect their elders.

One of the young guards had started to call him Harry the Hair.

He'd overheard the guard laughing about it to the female receptionist. To be fair, Harry knew it was his own fault – to a degree. He had made a point of telling the young man about the time he had spent in Cambodia many years back and how he had been told that bald men, like his good self, were revered, considered to possess wisdom.

He'd never been quite sure if the Cambodians had been having a laugh *with* him or *at* him. Still, he had liked the idea and it had stuck with him.

Harry had seen many changes in the Triangle area of the city, with businesses coming and going from the ramshackle old former mill. But throughout the ebb and flow of change, one constant remained. Or two, if you counted Harry himself. The streets of this run-down patch of the city seemed to have always been busy with a steady supply of women and cars. The women may have changed from time to time, with what seemed to be ever younger girls shivering a dance from one foot to another in the chill air. There were young men now too. That was new.

Despite the changes, Harry felt the atmosphere of seedy desperation always seemed to cling to the place. He wasn't sure if it came from the needs of the people who worked the streets. Their urgency to fuel drug habits, pay the rent or clothe their kids.

More likely it was the men who took advantage of what was on offer that made it feel so desperate to him.

He was no prude. He'd dabbled himself when he'd been off in far-away climes. But he had never been with any of the girls here. Not on your own doorstep was Harry's view on the matter. That was just cheap and tawdry. Plus, more chance of the wife finding out.

Still, he was bloody sick of being a skivvy.

Harry sighed knowing that if he didn't clean up then no-one would. He continued his circuit of the perimeter. Turning the corner, he came to an area frequented by patrons of the Triangle's nightlife.

It was a dead end street, tucked in to the side of his industrial unit. Tall blank brick walls rose up along the end and ran back up one side of street. The other side was afforded privacy by the presence of a dense hedge to the perimeter of a rarely used car park. A single streetlight offered the only glow of safety in this cut-off place. During the hours of darkness, it would cast a mean yellow glow over the street.

He smelt, then saw, the car. An older model, belching out exhaust fumes. The windows were misted up and the car hummed low and steady.

'Bloody hell.'

An exasperated Harry trudged over. He rapped his knuckles on the driver's window.

'Here mate, it's gone 7am, time to put it away and get home.'

There was no answer, but he could make out the vague shape of a figure inside.

The door was unlocked. As he opened it, a rush of moist heat hit his face. The man in the driver's seat looked like he was sleeping, head thrown back, mouth gaping open. But something felt wrong.

'Oi mate, had too much stress on the old ticker?'

Harry reached in and turned the engine off. He placed his fingers on the man's neck to check for a pulse.

Harry grunted. There it was, weak but evident.

Despite the warmth inside the car the man's skin was cool and clammy against his fingers. Withdrawing his hand, he rapidly wiped it against the leg of his uniform trousers.

'Stay with me mate, stay with me,' said Harry, and carefully closed the car door. He rushed back to his security desk, rang for help, and returned to keep an eye on the unconscious driver.

Harry opened the car door again. He prodded the driver's arm with one finger. No response. Harry tried again to locate the pulse. There it was, the faint tapping of it against his fingertips. It was a relief. At least the man was alive, even if barely from the look of things. He tried once more to stir the driver.

'Mate... hey mate, can you hear me?'

Still no response from the slumped figure. Harry noted that the man was older. Maybe late 60s, early 70s and dressed in slacks and a short-sleeved shirt. His belt and flies were undone. Leaning in Harry adjusted the man's clothing by flipping his shirt across the man's crotch.

'Least I can make you decent, mate'.

Harry spotted a black leather wallet lying in the driver's foot-well.

''Scuse me.'

He grasped the wallet between two fingers, before straightening up again.

'Okay, let's see who you are. Derek... Derek Foster. Right then, police will want to see this, I reckon.'

Sirens in the distance hailed the imminent arrival of help.

'Not long now Derek mate, they'll have you sorted soon.'

CHAPTER 3

Beth sat patiently in the clinic. She had arrived early today.

She had waited here, in this room, many times before.

It had been so often that she now knew most of the women who came for regular check-ups. Those who came to make sure they were clean, to allow them to carry on working. Those who came when the men had been more aggressive or had refused to use a condom.

There had been a wave of moving sexual health services into new accessible premises in community health clinics or even shopping centres. The clinic Beth was seated in was one of the last such services still to be within the grounds of a hospital.

The hospital was not exactly ashamed of providing the services of the clinic but then again, they didn't shout about it either. The place was tucked away in one of the older brick-built buildings at the rear of the grounds.

Beth didn't mind. She liked the character of the old place. Anyway, the place had been modernised inside. It was bright, cheery and clean.

Some effort had been made in the consultation room in which she was waiting to soften the more clinical nature of the space. Pot plants had been dotted along windowsills and a few colourful holiday postcards had been pinned to a cork notice board on one wall.

Other walls were decked with familiar eye-catching posters, with bold messages highlighting mental health, control and violence, unexpected pregnancy, Chlamydia, and other sexually transmitted diseases.

Funny how one way or another she seemed to have spent so much of her life being in this place.

The room door opened and Beth rose from her chair.

'Please do come in and take a seat,' she said.

A nervous-looking girl held herself back at the door.

'I'm Nurse Hooper, but please call me Beth. How can I help you today?'

The young girl, dressed simply in jeans and a loose black T-shirt, looked uncomfortably thin. Blonde hair was pulled back in a hard ponytail. The style accentuated the sharp line of the girl's cheekbones, above which worry showed in the girl's dark rimmed eyes.

Beth smiled warmly at the young woman, keen to put her at ease.

The girl shifted nervously and stepped forward to take a seat.

'Okay,' Beth started. 'I want you to know you can feel comfortable here, you can say whatever you like to me. My role is not to judge, but to help and support you, alright? So, do you want to tell me why you have come in today?'

The girl shuffled awkwardly. She perched on the edge of the chair. Her hands fluttered up to her head, smoothing her already tightly tamed hair.

Beth was reminded of an abandoned baby bird she had found at her father's house years ago. It had fallen from its nest and was flapping and squawking pathetically in a patch of tall grass. She had carefully picked it up and taken it into the house but despite her best efforts the poor creature had died in her hands.

'It's my boyfriend,' the girl said hesitantly. 'He wanted to be here, he had to take a phone call. Can we wait for him? He won't be long, I'm sure.'

Beth had seen it so many times before. Women came in with so called partners but the atmosphere was always so telling. Tense and prompted, the women would come to seek the medical help required but would be unwilling to engage with the staff's advice.

The undercurrent of control by the supposed boyfriends always seemed to be present at those awkward appointments.

It was odds on that this girl knew that Beth didn't believe her. Yet they both played along with the pretence. Sometimes it wasn't worth rocking the boat. Especially when it appeared likely that the women would come off worse once the couple had left the clinic.

Beth wanted to take advantage of this time alone with the young woman. Maybe there was a chance she could get her to open up.

'Well yes, we could wait a little while, but we've got a really busy clinic today, so it might be best if we at least started our discussion. I'll tell you what, let's just begin and see how we get on. He can always join us when he's finished his call can't he?'

The girl's hands were clasped tightly. White knuckles and a knot of twisted fingers that she was pressing down against her knees. They bounced vigorously as she nervously jigged her legs up and down. She glanced back to the door, then gave a tight smile.

The girl looked so incredibly young. Too young to be doing what Beth felt sure she was being made to do. The sheen of makeup she wore couldn't hide the truth from a practiced eye.

Gently does it, thought Beth.

She proceeded to talk through the various services the clinic offered, looking for a spark in the girl that would lead her to the exact reason for the visit. Eventually the girl relaxed a little. She even gave her name: Leah.

Beth was showing her a relevant website when the ping of her mobile made Leah stiffen. The girl hunched forward once more, pulling the phone from her pocket.

Beth busied herself creating an information pack for Leah to take with her. She pushed a handful of condoms into a small carrier with some leaflets. She glanced over at Leah tapping away at her phone.

The girl looked downright miserable.

'Right then, Leah,' said Beth brightly, 'here's a little light reading for you.'

Leah looked up at her, the angle made her dark eyes look large and sunken. Like a frightened animal.

'I've got to go,' she said curtly.

'Okay, no problem Leah. You know where I am if you need more advice, or if you need to just, you know, talk.'

Leah's features softened a little. 'Thanks, I appreciate it. I really do, but I have to go.'

'Take care then.'

The girl hurriedly grabbed the carrier bag and left the room.

Beth sat for some time staring into space. The evident age of the girl and her fragile state lingered. Beth could not shake off a deep sense of concern for her wellbeing.

Sometimes just seeing people here didn't seem enough. She had talked to her manager Jenny about this already without much joy.

'We're just too busy, Beth,' she'd said. 'We can't do *everything* for *everyone*. I know it's tough seeing the damage people do to their lives, but we aren't here to save them. They have to do that themselves. We can only do so much and they often get themselves into these situations, then don't do enough to get themselves out. They need to take some personally responsibility for their lives.'

Beth did not agree. She acknowledged individual accountability, but people got into bad situations for all sorts of reasons. There were plenty of vulnerable people who had been coerced. Those damaged by experiences that ended up selling themselves for sex. It was never a one-size-fits-all scenario.

No, Beth wasn't sure yet what to do about Leah. She had to do something though. Beth just needed to figure out what that was.

CHAPTER 4

A decent, upright citizen, he had prided himself on that.

To his wife, neighbours and down at his club, Derek was a man of honour. You could rely on Derek Foster to do the right thing.

Yet each man has at least one weakness and Mrs Foster was no longer interested in that particular part of their relationship. Yet there were still urges and they needed attention. Even at what Derek admitted to be an advanced stage of his life, there remained a desire to be touched in that certain way. To be caressed, with at least the pretence of desire from a woman. Plus, the rest, if he could get it.

The only option he had found was to cruise the Triangle.

At first there had been trepidation. Then guilt. Lots of guilt. Over time though, Derek had found a way to let that go. Or at least squash it deep inside himself. The pleasure, the relief had taken over. He found the excitement addictive. It was like some kind of game. He knew what he wanted; they knew it too.

He would drive around the area, voyeuristically at first. Eventually the car would slow as he made his selection. Never the older one though. On those occasions he had selected company from the few mature ladies, he had found that his mind had drifted uncomfortably to thoughts of Mrs Foster.

That just would not do.

Plus, the firm flesh of youth added a further charge of excitement to the engagements.

Being of an ordered mind, Derek had worked out a procedure for these encounters. After the looking and the selection came the thrill of the girl sliding into the car seat next to him. Then came the drive, to find a quiet spot in which to park up for their liaison.

Derek had known it was somewhat foolish to use such romantic terminology as 'liaison' for such a transaction, but it was part of his personal code. He liked to believe that he treated all the women he used respectfully. He prided himself on being cordial to them, engaging in small talk before the main event, being mindful of their physical comfort throughout. Remembering to be gracious and thankful after.

He frequently found sleep hard to gain. Age, he guessed. That and the familiar physical frustration.

It was no different that night. He had dozed fitfully and it would soon be dawn. Careful not to disturb Mrs Foster and with considerable stealth for a man of his years, he exited the bed. Dressing himself downstairs, Derek crept from the house.

Starting the car was tricky. He sat for a few moments, the engine running and observed the house. No lights blinked on; no curtains twitched open. He felt safe to continue.

The car had seemed to know where he wanted to go, they had travelled this route so often together.

Driving through the Triangle, he had quickly spotted an appealing looking woman. This was someone new, a girl he had not seen before.

Derek felt a heightened excitement. Cosseted in the safe darkness of his warm car as he watched the new girl from a distance. She was tall, slender and he had been able to make out the sheen of long pale hair cascading down her back. The girl had turned on her heels and paused. She appeared to be staring right back at him.

Derek held his breath. He was deeply intrigued. Yes, she had definitely looked at him. He saw her raise one hand than place it on her waist pushing her hip out towards him. Derek dropped the car into gear and slowly rolled it towards her.

'Good evening, my dear.'

'Alright mate. You looking for some company?'

Derek decided he enjoyed the tradition of the introduction as much as the elicit act itself. Well almost. It added yet more thrill to the game.

'Well yes, I think I am. Are you free to accompany me to somewhere a little more discrete?'

Derek smiled at his own politeness, but to have been rude to the girl would have been unthinkable for him. The girl in turn had been a little abrupt he thought, but then, he had reflected, she must deal with a lot of uncouth types.

'Yeah, sure,' had been her simple response.

She slid smoothly into the passenger seat next to him. Derek caught a waft of her perfume. Sickly sweet, something cheap no doubt from the market or off a supermarket shelf, he thought. He had found he didn't actually mind. It just added to the tone of the experience. He glanced at her, taking in the soft sheen of her bare thighs in the half light. The girl just looked straight ahead.

'Shall we go?' she said flatly.

'Why of course, my dear. Let me just get the car into gear.'

They had driven a little around the quiet streets, passing other girls on other beats who quickly dropped their hands and poses once they spotted the girl in the car with him.

Finally, Derek turned off the main roads and pulled the car into the forecourt of a dilapidated block of garages. Most of them were no longer in use and gaped open like blackened teeth in a grimace. The odd one here and there still seem to have their doors intact suggesting that they were in use, probably for some illegal purpose, Derek surmised.

'Not here.'

'But I always... I mean, I have been told this is a quiet spot.'

The girl had turned to face him. She was barely visible in the diminished light, but Derek detected the hard line of her mouth.

'I said not here.'

He felt the pressure of her gaze. Intense. She was certainly a stern one. Still, he didn't mind that really. In fact, it was rather a turn-on.

'It's too dark here. I won't be able to see what I'm doing.'

'Oh, I understand.' Derek nodded.

'Nor will you.'

'Yes, I see. Alright my dear, you tell me where.'

The girl had directed Derek to a nearby street lit by the softness of a single streetlamp. It was an area he was unfamiliar with, close to a dense privet hedge on the edge of what he took to be an industrial park.

He pulled the car over to the kerb and moved to turn off the engine. The girl reached out a hand and firmly squeezed his thigh.

'No. Leave the engine running.'

'Okay my dear, as you wish.'

Derek had been a little surprised by her request but did as he was bid, enjoying the sensation of her fingers gripping his leg. She had started to run her hand vigorously up and down his trouser leg, pushing the fabric such that it rubbed pleasantly against his skin.

'I –' he attempted.

'Shhh.'

Unbuckling his belt, she deftly pulled down his zip.

'But the money –'

'Shhh. It's fine. Later.'

He gasped with pleasure as her hand slide down inside the waistband of his trousers to caress his growing erection through the thin cotton of his boxer shorts.

Derek closed his eyes, enjoying her touch. They hadn't even discussed what he wanted, but she was just so forceful. That in itself was extremely thrilling and it wouldn't take her long to get him to climax, he was sure of that.

He became aware of her shuffling round in the car seat and he opened his eyes a little wondering if she was about to use her mouth on him. He certainly hoped so. She still had one hand gripped around him through his underwear and he dearly wanted her to set him free from the confines of his clothing. Derek reached down to try to pull his pants down to allow her greater access.

'No!' she had barked sharply. 'I will do it.'

Derek relented. 'I am in your hands my dear, quite literally.'

Finally, she freed him from the clothing that had tightened around his groin and he felt the warm skin of her fingers against his hardened flesh.

He found then he could relax a little again and closed his eyes momentarily, focusing on the sensation. There would be plenty of time to look when she had those soft full lips around him. The headiness of her perfume had increased and he felt the warmth of her body as she moved closer to him. Derek's heart was pounding and his breathing shortened with excitement. He was going to enjoy this one.

'Ow! Bloody hell!'

A sharp pain in his arm abruptly pulled him back from the brink.

'What the hell have you done?'

Looking down, Derek could see a shiny tube in the girl's hand. A drop of blood had beaded on his skin of his left arm. It broke free and ran warmly in a dark bracelet around his elbow.

A needle. The stupid girl had stuck him with damn needle!

Christ, what had she done to him? Why? He tried to struggle, to reach out to her but she seemed to be moving away from him.

He felt like he was falling backwards. An unknown darkness was welcoming him, rolling itself around him. It didn't matter. He couldn't even try to resist it. Nothing mattered anymore. He simply needed to embrace the obscurity.

CHAPTER 5

'Do we have a name?' asked Triage Nurse Dan Glenn.

'This is Derek Foster, we radioed his status through,' replied the paramedic, as he smoothly assisted the nursing staff to move Derek Foster's unconscious body from the ambulance gurney to a bed in the resuscitation area.

'He was found unconscious in his car, in the red-light area. Breathing is very shallow. His slow respiration rate coupled with lots of gurgling in his throat suggests fluid in the lungs. Also, heart rate is low, as is his body temperature and his pupils have been constricted on every check. We think he's probably taken something, there's a bloodied puncture mark and bruising on his left arm.'

'Thanks, that's really helpful, we'll take it from here.'

Nurse Glenn bustling round, starting his own assessment of the prone man.

Derek Foster was in a coma. His breathing was barely perceptible and his blood pressure was dangerously low. A bluish tinge had settled over his lips and fingertips and his skin felt clammy to Dan Glenn's touch.

'What do we have here then, nurse?'

Dan was interrupted in his administrations by the arrival of the consultant, Doctor Khan. He brought with him his usually silent entourage of student medics.

'Hello, Doctor Khan. I think this is maybe a slightly unusual one. It is possible that this could be a heroin overdose or maybe even morphine. I believe he was found in some disarray down the Triangle, I reckon someone down there has given him something.'

'Really nurse? Morphine? I can see heroin as being a possibility, particularly if he's been spending time down in that particular part of town, but morphine?'

'Well yes, Doctor, I know it's unusual but don't you remember that case last month? It seems kind of similar to this one. Hang on, let me get the file up.'

Glenn and Khan moved to the nurse's station to access a computer terminal. The students dutifully shuffled after them, to huddle behind, peering at the record Dan Glenn was tapping into the machine.

'Ah, here we are, yes... Malcolm Smith, aged 74, admitted on the 3rd of last month, unconscious with a needle mark in his left arm, he died shortly after admission, whilst still in A&E.'

The doctor looked over Glenn's shoulder at the notes on the screen.

'Well yes, it does seem similar and the bloods did show a very high level of morphine in his system,' Khan said begrudgingly.

'I think nothing was made of it because Mr Smith had been long known to us here as a drug user. He has notes as long as your arm, having been admitted so many times over the years, all drug related. The thing that stuck in my mind from this was the morphine though. The presence of it, I mean, and the level identified in the bloods results. Yeah, I know it's unusual, but it is a known street drug. Even for a man of his age and vast narcotics experience its uncommon. But who knows? Maybe he was at a point in his life where he just didn't care what he was taking. He was getting on a bit and you can only abuse your body like that for so long.'

'Well, I'm not sure it up to us to make such a value judgement on Mr Smith's lifestyle choice. However, I agree that it is a little outside of the norm for what we have come to expect from this age group. I know that, as you say, morphine is used as a street drug sometimes and some people will use anything, they can get their hands on. Maybe we are behind the times here, eh? Its use could well be more common now than we realised.'

'Yeah, but I still think it's kinda unusual for two men of these sorts of ages? Yeah, pensioners aren't what they used to be. We all know working here that it's not all pipe and slippers when you get to that age these days. But these circumstances? There's still something off about it. Look here, the police report says Malcolm Smith was found in his car down in the Triangle. So that's two elderly men taking fatal levels of morphine via injections to their left arms and in the red-light district? It could be a total coincidence, but to me, well there's something weird about that. It's just a gut reaction of course but –'

Glenn shrugged and looked questioningly at the doctor.

Doctor Khan raised an eye-brow and ran his fingers along his jaw line, scratching at his beard.

'Hmm, yes well maybe you are on to something, Nurse Glenn,' he mused. 'Okay, we'll let the police know about your thoughts on the matter. Yes?'

Dan Glen nodded, pleased to have received support from the consultant. Doctor Khan could be a bit severe at times and was certainly hard on his students, but it was only because he wanted the best for his patient. Dan respected that.

He watched with some amusement as the Consultant wandered off the next bay, herding his gaggle of young medics with a raised hand and a flick of the wrist.

Despite Dan Glenn's best efforts, within the hour, Derek Foster had lost the battle with the drug and his life.

*

The reception area of the Accident and Emergency Department was heaving when Detective Inspector Abby Davidson arrived. She always felt that these places were more like corridors than actual hospital departments. Nothing more than long convoluted lines of small rooms off twisting, never-ending passageways. Quite often these days the corridors would also be lined with patients lying awkwardly on gurneys, as they awaited a free consultation room or ward bed.

Such is the state of the NHS, thought Abby Davidson with some sadness.

Some rooms had solid doors, but many others just had curtains and she could hear the low hum of conversations and the groans of patients within them. She wasn't too happy with her boss for sending her on a job that could have been handled by uniform. She hadn't joined CID for this.

Sometimes Detective Chief Inspector Peter Bloom was a law unto himself. Abby smiled at her own pun.

He did get results though and there was always a method in there, somewhere. Even if that was often a mystery to her at the start.

She located the reception desk and was directed to the nurse's station.

'I'm looking for Nurse Glenn.'

'That's me,' said a nurse turning from the monitor he had been typing at.

'I'm DI Abby Davidson, you called us about two recent deaths that you had suspicions over?'

'Oh, I was expecting the usual uniformed officer. Is there something special going on with this that we should know about?'

Abby Davidson sighed and allowed a light smile to flash across her lips. 'Yes, I'm sure you were, but anything connected to the Triangle and my Governor wants to know what's going on, so here I am –'

Nurse Glenn held up his hands in mock surrender. 'Oh no, I'm not complaining, it's fine by me, just pleased to see that you're all paying attention to what goes on down there.'

'Okay, let me in on what you think are the similarities of the two cases.'

Malcolm Smith had been what some might call a 'character' on his estate and had been well known to the police. Abby wasn't surprised to hear that he had died. She was more surprised that he had lived as long as he had, given his chosen lifestyle. Bloom had once told her that Malcolm had been a rock musician in his former years. He had only ever achieved local notoriety, but it seemed he had never quite shaken off the accessories of that kind of existence.

Abby had listened intently, focused on the details the nurse was providing. When Nurse Glenn had finished, she nodded her head a little with a small perfunctory smile.

'Okay, so I can see that the cause of death was the same, but Malcolm Smith was something of, well... a lowlife, to put it bluntly. He had a rap sheet for drug offences that span decades. They seem to be very different men with probably vastly different lifestyles. Maybe there is as you suggest, a connection. I'm just not seeing it yet.'

'Look, I realise that Malcolm Smith was a heavy drug user and had been for years, from what I heard he saw himself as some sort of Howard Marks figure.'

'More like some sink estate wannabe.'

'Well, maybe a mixture of the two.'

'Hmm, dunno about that.'

'Okay, but look, we are getting off the point.'

Abby nodded allowing Nurse Glenn to continue.

'So that's why we never thought his death was suspicious at the time. It seemed more like an accident, like he'd experimented with the wrong drug or his body had finally had enough of the cocktail he fed it. But the thing is that, well, they're both men.'

Abby Davidson raised one eyebrow. Nurse Glenn was quick to speak again. 'Bear with me. What I'm saying is, they might have been old, but they were still blokes, if you catch my drift. They were both down at the Triangle for some company, you know? Plus, they both died as a result of having high doses of morphine in their systems. I know it can be an abused drug but still, something just doesn't feel right here. It's a combination of their ages, them being such different men, the type of drugs and the fact that they were both found in a very similar state down at the Triangle.'

Nurse Glenn was forceful in his view and Abby found herself willing to run with it. 'I do see your point there. Leave it with me and I'll look into it further.'

She turned to go.

'And thanks nurse, you'd make a pretty decent detective you know,' she said over her shoulder. 'I'll see you tonight, yeah?'

'Yeah, I'm cooking so don't be late. Hopefully, we will have the flat to ourselves –'

Nurse Glenn blew her a kiss.

'Sounds good to me.'

She sashayed out of view and Dan Glenn returned his attention to the Nurse's Station. He always enjoyed the little game of professionalism they played whenever she turned up on official business. In an odd way it was kind of like role-playing and added a certain excitement to their work-life engagements.

'Alright Dan.'

Nurse Glenn was abruptly broken away from his musing about the spicier side of his and Abby's relationship. His friend Josh Simpson was now standing behind him.

'Woah, Josh... where did you come from? Don't bleedin' sneak up on me like that, I thought you were the police back again.'

Josh Simpson laughed. 'Sorry mate, just here to do some interviews for my latest piece. You know the one I mentioned last week about the decriminalisation down the Triangle?'

He didn't wait for the nurse to respond.

'I was hoping to catch some of the Sexual Health Clinic staff for comments. Just thought I'd call in to see you as well, mate. So, what have the police been here for then?'

Dan Glenn folded his arms and gave his friend a hard look.

'Mate, you know I can't tell you that. Jesus, you're always looking for the next scoop for that dirty rag of a newspaper, aren't you? Surely there's enough down the Triangle to go at without hassling me? It's like the flamin' Wild West down there these days.'

'Ha-ha, yeah it's not quite that bad you know, but Dan come on, be a mate, help me out. I'll make it worth your while –'

Nurse Glenn retained a veneer of stoic resilience.

Josh Simpson tried again.

'Look, when have I ever put you in a dodgy situation, eh? You're my source here, aren't you? And I go out of my way to protect my sources, don't I?'

'Oh right, is that what I am? A minute ago, I was your mate, but now I'm just another source.'

'We *are* mates, fella, of course we are. It's just that, well... you work here, don't you, and I am duty bound to report matters of interest to the public.'

'Yeah, well you can salve your conscious any old way you like Josh, but I've still got a job to do here.'

Josh smiled broadly at his friend.

'Okay mate, okay. Relax. Just give us a little clue then.'

Dan sighed. Josh was tenacious, he gave him that. He clearly wasn't going to leave him alone unless he gave him at least one small titbit of information. Dan reluctantly gave in.

'Alright, well you know what you said about why you are here?'

'Yeah.'

'It's about something that's gone on down there.'

'What, you mean at the Triangle?'

Dan nodded.

'So, what is it about the Triangle? What's happened down there now?'

'Look, I told you I can't say.'

Despite his statement, Dan side-stepped, allowing Josh a momentary glance at the screen behind him. Malcolm Smith's record was still laid out on it in clear view. The nurse quickly flicked off the screen.

'Fuck, I could lose my job for letting you see that.'

Josh could see how much this was stressing his friend out but the journalist in him couldn't let it lie.

'I see. Something about him and the Triangle. But what though?'

'Look, I'm not telling you anything else, Josh. Fuck off now and let me get back to work. I've got a lot of patients to see, you know.'

'Yeah mate, sorry. Okay, I'm off, but just one last question. Just nod or shake your head, but is this about how he died down there?'

Glenn gave an almost imperceptible twitch of his head causing his chin to bob down. It was enough for Josh.

'Cheers, Dan. See you later.'

Josh headed back the way he had arrived. He knew there was a germ of a story here. He could just feel it. A bit more research and he would have an idea of what was going on. But first he needed to try to get those interviews.

'Well, well, well. What are you doing here?'

Looking up he saw that DI Abby Davidson had stepped in front of him. She had her hands on her hips and was cocking her head to one side. That posture always gave her attitude. He couldn't help but grin at her.

'I don't need a smile from you, Mr Simpson. I need to know why you're here.'

Josh laughed. 'I'm just visiting Dan is all. Are you guys going to be in the flat tonight?'

Abby Davidson regarded Josh coolly and then broke into a smile of her own.

'Yeah, I think so, Dan said he would cook tonight.'

'Okay, cool. I'll probably go out then, give you two lovebirds some "alone time". If you know what I mean.'

Abby laughed.

'Well, that's uncommonly decent of you, Josh. Thanks, I might see you before you go out then. Laters.'

She didn't buy that he had just popped into see Dan. The detective in her pondered on the possible reasons he could have for being here, roaming the corridors of the hospital. But in fairness he was Dan's flat mate, so she would let it go, for now.

'Yeah, see you.'

Josh was relieved to see her move towards the main exit doors of the building. He liked Abby a lot. It was best to, seeing as she was his flatmate's girlfriend. Easier too as well, as she never could seem to turn off that copper's head of hers. Bit like him, really. He knew a workaholic when he saw one and he was forever open and alert for new stories and leads. That's what made him the good, persistent journalist he was.

CHAPTER 6

Josh wound his way through the labyrinthic corridors. He exited the building. The sky had darkened since he had arrived at the hospital and he hurried across the hospital grounds, keen to dodge a potential soaking.

Signs told him that he had located the Sexual Health Clinic in its secluded spot, on the edge of the hospital estate.

Even in these so-called liberated times, who wants to be seen coming and going from the Clap Clinic? he thought.

Society may have come a long way in some matters, but when it came to sex, most of us were still like kids giggling at the back of the class. We either didn't take it seriously or we were too embarrassed to face up to it.

Well, someone needed to be grown up about it and that someone was Josh Simpson. He laughed at his own pomposity. Still, he did have a job to do. Right then, who could he speak to, he wondered?

He halted abruptly at the sight of DI Abby Davidson entering the clinic.

'Damn it,' he muttered. 'Why hasn't she left the hospital yet?'

Josh was unsure of what to do. If he went in, she would want to know why he was there. He could do without her interference. Best to leave it for now. It would only wind her up and she was already in full on PC Plod mode. She might think he was following her around to chase a story as well.

He was of course doing just that, but Abby was one of the last people he wanted aware of that fact. She would suss him straight away on that one.

He was disappointed, but there was always another opportunity. He wasn't about to give up. He could smell that there was something worth investigating here. He would be back.

*

In the clinic reception, DI Davidson was asking if she could check a couple of names. The receptionist Lucy sighed. She had the practiced expression of someone used to dealing with the oddest of questions.

'I'm sure you know the drill, Officer. That information is confidential. You have to go through the proper channels.'

Abby plastered on what she hoped was her most approachable smile.

'Yes of course, but sometimes, when matters are urgent your colleagues have been able to help us out.'

Lucy sniffed and hammered down firmly on her computer keyboard. 'Well, that's not what my manager has said to me.' She was a stickler for protocol. 'We have patient confidentiality to think of. The matters that people come in here for, well... it's all very much of a sensitive nature. I am sure you can see that we can't just be handing out information at the drop of a hat. As I said, there is a procedure to follow.'

'Well yes, I realise that, but I am here on official police business.'

'Yes, and in that case, you will know the procedure that I am referring to very well. You will know how to follow it to the letter, I am sure.'

Lucy made it abundantly clear that she was returning her full attention to the monitor in front of her. She started to type vigorously once more, her fingers falling hard on the keys, causing them to clatter loudly.

Abby stood for a moment staring at her. The receptionist continued to pointedly ignore her. Eventually, a frustrated Abby,

32

realising she wasn't about to get any further with this approach, feigned giving up.

She sighed heavily and Lucy craned to gaze even more intently at her screen.

It really wasn't getting Abby anywhere. She backed off, weaved her way through the reception room chairs towards the exit. She looked back quickly around the room and spotted Beth Hooper's head, popping out from one of the consultation room doors leading off the reception area.

Beth appeared to be scanning the room, evidently looking for her next patient. Abby took this as an opportunity. Raising one hand she moved to follow Beth back into the side room.

Lucy looked up. It was too late.

'Excuse me. Hey!'

But her call was ineffectual. Beth had already closed the consultation room door and Abby had gained access.

Beth gestured for Abby to take a seat.

'Hello, I'm Nurse Beth Hooper and how can I help you today?'

'Hi I'm Abby, Abby Davidson.'

Beth nodded and smiled encouragingly waiting for Abby to proceed. Abby thought there was something vaguely familiar about the name Beth Hooper, but she just couldn't place it. She had barely had any time to decide how to play this one. Maybe a straight bat would best here.

'Look,' she started, 'I will come clean.'

Beth looked at her again reassuringly.

'I'm actually not here for a consultation, I'm from the police.' She had been reaching into her pocket as she spoke. She now presented her warrant card for Beth's perusal.

'I'm just after some information about a couple of people that may or may not have visited the clinic here.'

Beth was immediately wary, but she thought she might as well play along a little, at least see where this was headed. Always best to try to keep one step ahead with the police, in her experience.

'Why do you think they might have been patients here?'

'Well, you know the Triangle area?'

'Yes, I am aware of it.'

'Well, how can I put this; they were purchasers of activities down there.'

'What exactly do you mean by activities?'

'I mean they paid sex workers for their services down there.'

Beth nodded. Still not willing to give anything away. 'I see.'

'We are trying to obtain some background information on the two persons in question.'

'Well, I'm sure Lucy will have told you we do not share patient information just like that. You need to request it in the official way.'

Abby was a little irked that she was again failing to make progress. The nurse seemed to be afflicted with the same 'by the book' approach as the receptionist. Were they all such damn jobsworths here?

In a way, she could understand why they would be. To be fair she had been called one her-self at times by others back at the station. Still, she was trying to broaden her skills and abilities when it came to investigating cases and that meant stepping outside of protocol, doing things differently sometimes. Time to up the ante a little, she thought.

'Look Nurse Hooper. What I am investigating, well, these could be potential murders.'

Beth must have allowed shock to momentarily wash over her face as the police officer now wore a look of acknowledgement. Abby knew she had made some kind of in-road, even if it was just a small chink. She began warming to her theme.

'I don't know if you have ever been down to that area of the city, but it's rough. Not a very nice place for women to be, or for some men it seems. There's a vast array of nefarious activities that are going on that are of concern to us. We just want to try to get to the bottom of some of them and try to make it a safer place.

You must see the girls that work down there? They must come to the clinic for their check-ups and stuff, yeah? So maybe some of them have talked about what's going on down there?'

'If they have it hasn't been to me.'

'Really? Okay, well do you ever go down there? To see them in an outreach capacity?'

'No, not generally. It's been years since I've been down there.'

'But you have been down there then?'

'Yes, as I said, years ago. I haven't been anywhere near the Triangle recently.'

'Not in a professional capacity?'

Beth was beginning to get annoyed at this prying. Just what was this detective trying to get at here?

'Well, no, as I said it was years ago, before I was a nurse.'

'I see, so why were you down there then?'

Beth stood up. 'Look, I really don't see what relevance that has to your initial line of questioning. Please, I have patients waiting and you really need to leave now.'

Abby was annoyed with herself for overstepping the mark. She had just got a little carried away with her questioning. Once she started it was often difficult to stop. It could end up looking like she was just being personally intrusive. Beth's defensiveness about having been down to the Triangle in the past had piqued her interest though. One to explore later, she ruminated as she stood to leave.

'Well, thank you for your time Nurse Hooper.' She dropped her card on to Beth's desk. 'There's my number, should anything come to mind that you think might help us.'

Beth nodded and began to straighten a pile of files with her back to the room. Abby took this as her sign to leave.

She would be back, even if it had to be through a lengthier red tape route. There was definitely more to know here.

*

Back at the police station Abby quickly searched for past misdemeanours for both men. Nothing came up for Derek Foster, but Malcolm had lived enough life to exhaust two or even three men. Still, it was odd that Derek Foster had been found in a similar situation to Malcolm Smith, particularly in respect of the drugs in his system.

She could really do with talking this out with Bloom. It would help to get it all straight in her head before she delved any deeper.

Abby looked out across the open plan office and tried to spot her boss's head above one of the computer terminals. The days of teetering stacks of paper files were long gone now that just about everything was stored electronically. All the better for it in Abby's view. Not that she was some kind of eco-warrior or something, but she was not a fan of working in the midst of clutter and couldn't abide waste.

There was no sign of him at any of the desks in her eye line. Not much more she could do at this stage then. Abby reluctantly set the task aside. Her attention returned to her other duties. Always plenty of reports to write up and this matter, well it wasn't going to go away easily. There would be opportunity to revisit it and soon.

CHAPTER 7

Malcolm, or Mal to his friends, liked to imagine himself to have been there, done that.

'Pretty much done the lot, me,' he was prone to boasting.

He had certainly tried his very best to smoke it, swallow it, snort it and inject it all over the years. Revelled in it too. A self-created notoriety as some kind of fallen rock star with a colourful past.

It was true that he had been in a couple of bands as a young man, but he'd never been what could be termed a competent musician. The truth of it was that music had been a means to an end for him.

What Malcolm had really been interested in was getting high and in as many ways as possible. As a result, Malcolm had been a regular visitor to the Triangle for years, decades. His main drug of choice, particularly in his later years, was weed. At this stage in his life when it came to the "old narcotics" he had grown ever more particular about what he ingested.

Despite his offbeat appearance, or maybe because of it, in some of the circles he frequented he'd been viewed with suspicion. He'd even been accused of being an undercover cop. That had given him a laugh. It didn't help that he had a habit of showing up unannounced at dealers' doors to introduced himself. But once the hard stares and aggressive posturing was dealt with and he'd cut through the crap, deals had been made.

What he was though, was persistent in his goal for top draw drugs. Once he gained the trust of some of the best providers, they in turn became more than happy for him to buy what was on offer. The fact was that Malcolm was used to getting what he wanted, even if he had to sweet talk a little to get it.

As for the other pleasures the Triangle offered, Malcolm did occasionally allow himself to feed his libido alongside his drug habit. He took no shame in availing himself of the services of the women who worked the streets down there. Even in his later years he still felt that spark in his loins, maybe not as much and he certainly couldn't last as long as he used to, but it was still there.

He couldn't help but spot them as he wandered or drove through the streets of an evening. It seemed like they were on every street corner trying to catch his eye.

Well, Malcolm had thought, *a man has needs, don't he?*

Even an old timer like himself. So why not?

Malcolm had always been someone who didn't think too deeply about the consequences of his actions on others. It wasn't that he didn't care. It was more that he didn't want to care. If he had cared, it would have affected his buzz and he couldn't have that.

He knew some of the girls had been brought here from other countries, possibly against their will. There was also a really good chance that none of the girls wanted to be out selling themselves on the streets. But for Malcolm, that - in a twisted way - only added to his own thrill.

Selfish of him yes, but he was a man who liked to experience life not think about it, and it was ultimately this *laissez faire* attitude that led to his death in the Triangle.

It was a new one that had caught his eye the night he died. She had sort of looked familiar to him, but he couldn't quite place her. Not that it mattered; he just wanted to fuck her.

'Evening, darling.'

'Hi, you looking for business?'

Malcolm laughed. 'I'm looking to try you out.'

'What? I don't know what you're on about, do you want company or not?'

'Yes love, forgive me, I do, indeed I do.'

'You trying to be clever or summat?'

'No no love, it's just my sense of humour.'

'Whatever, as long as you're paying.'

'And I am, sweet girl.'

The car was his home from home. He'd filled it with the debris of his life. He clumsily grabbed a pile of old tape cassettes and CDs from the passenger seat. Their plastic cases slipped against each other and he awkwardly threw them over his shoulder into the back of the vehicle. A rigid-looking waxed canvas jacket followed and landing upright on the seat, like a half man perched on the backseat.

The jacket had seen many a pub and party floor and carried a myriad of rips and stains to show it. He wasn't surprised that it could sit up on its own; hell, if he put it in a front seat it could probably drive the car for him, or at least ride shotgun and navigate for him. The thought made him chuckle.

'What's so funny?'

The girl sounded annoyed again. Bit of an attitude this one, he decided.

'Nothing, love. Sorry, it's nothing. Just a daft old man, thinking daft old thoughts. Please, get in won't you?'

He had pushed the door open allowing the inside light to illuminate the car's interior. The girl eyed the remaining layer of rubbish in the foot well. Empty cigarette packets and torn remnants of Rizla papers intermingled with sweet wrappers and the shiny pyramids of empty plastic sandwich boxes.

'There you go, fit for a princess.'

She sniffed. 'Don't know about that.'

But without further hesitation, she clambered in next to him.

'I'm Mal, and you are very lovely. What's your name?'

Her legs were bare beneath a short dark skirt. He couldn't resist reaching out to stroke the soft firm flesh of her thigh. The skin was smooth and cool under his touch.

'Hey!' she snapped. 'You haven't paid yet.'

'Okay, okay. Sorry love, you are just so gorgeous I can't help myself.'

'Well try, and you don't need to know my name. Call me whatever you like, I really don't care.'

The girl really did seem rather bad tempered and Malcolm wondered if he had made a poor choice this time. He knew they often didn't want to be here with him in his grotty old car, but he liked them to at least pretend that they did. He didn't want her attitude putting a dampener on what he was paying for.

'Drive over to that dead end up there.'

The girl gestured to him.

Malcolm nodded and proceeded as instructed. He wanted to keep her sweet and get his money's worth. There was a chance her aggressive manner meant she didn't mind having it rough. His luck might be in after all.

The dead end was between two tall brick walls under the viaduct. A large stone boulder had been placed in the road ahead. The viaduct walls were angled here, such that it was difficult to see beyond the boulder in either direction along the closed road. Behind them, the road was lined with derelict buildings, their broken windows devoid of light or activity. They were very much alone in this secluded spot.

'Right, shall we get down to business?'

The girl shifted in her seat and leaned towards Malcolm. He felt her hand on his thigh.

He was somewhat surprised. After all, she had rebuked him only moments ago for touching her leg before they had agreed a price.

'Don't you want to talk money first?'

The girl didn't respond other than to squeeze his thigh harder and slide her hand further up his leg. Malcolm's excitement level accelerated steeply. Maybe she wanted him, genuinely wanted him and maybe she wanted it. Hard. A good rough fuck. Her hand and the thought of what she might do to him, let him do to her, was making him harder than he'd managed in years.

She moved her hand to his groin, still squeezing.

Malcolm drew in a sharp breath. Fuck. This was so exciting. He thought he might actually come now.

Only wait.

No.

That was starting to hurt him.

Surely, she knew how tender those areas of a man could be, even when aroused? She was squeezing just that bit too hard now.

'Hey love, ease off a bit, that's too much.'

He reached to grip her hand, trying to lever her fingers off him.

'I said, leave go, you're fucking hurting me.'

His hand closed fully around her slender arm and he was surprised that his forefinger and thumb could meet around her wrist. He tried to make a joke. Maybe if he lightened the mood, she would ease back a little.

'You got a right good grip for a girl with proper skinny arms love, my cock is fatter than that.'

'It won't be when I've finished with it,' she retorted.

He was unsure if her tone was a come on or a threat. The whole thing was happening way too fast and he was struggling to get a handle on just what was going on. He could tell, even in the reduced light that she was looking directly at him. Man, she was strong! She still hadn't let go despite his efforts and she was smiling oddly at him. The half-light picked out the white of her teeth and the hard edges of her bones structure. It made her look not quite human. Menacing.

Malcolm felt afraid.

He tried again to remove her grip, using both hands now to ease her off finger by finger. Then suddenly a small flash of something moving towards him.

She had something in her other hand. A needle, and she had stuck him with it.

'What the fuck! What's in that? Fuck, get off me –'

She was silent.

Why didn't she bloody well answer him? He needed to know what she was injecting him with, so he could be prepared for it to hit.

He struggled against her grip. The point of the needle was now firmly embedded in his arm. His exertions did nothing to assist his position. Quite the opposite in fact. The tussle between them had allowed her to drive the needle deeper into his flesh. It was now a simple matter for her to quickly depress the plunger into the needle, pushing its contents into his bloodstream.

He felt the rush immediately, knew it too.

Felt like a downer, was it heroin? Maybe, but, bloody hell, why?

No time to ponder further as Malcolm slumped back in his seat. The girl finally released her grip on him. He was drifting now, riding the drug as it coursed through him.

He watched her lean over to lift his eyelids wider. She was smiling darkly. He could see the tip of her tongue caught between her teeth as she dropped her chin in a little nod of satisfaction.

Malcolm closed his eyes. Just for a moment.

God... this woman was mad, and he was in serious danger. But what had become more important was an intense need for a good long sleep. Yeah, that would sort him out.

But what about the girl? He forced his heavy eyelids open again.

He was alone now, still in the car. Alone in the dark, in this remote, quiet place.

It felt okay though. He knew that was the drug's doing, giving him an emotional blanket to dampen his fears. But damn, it felt good and he was so very tired. He mentally pulled the blanket closer around himself. Time to rest.

CHAPTER 8

Beth kept replaying the consultation session with the girl, Leah. The young woman had seemed worryingly vulnerable. Yet was she being too judgmental?

Beth shook her head. No. Leah had clearly been trying her best to look mature. To affect a mask that was beyond her years, but her demeanour told the truth.

A knot of anxiety was forming, twisting in Beth's belly. One of these situations she wasn't going to be able to leave alone. This would mean visiting the Triangle. Not an appealing thought at the best of times. The knot tightened inside her at the thought of returning to that place. Yet she must.

Grabbing her coat and bag, Beth steeled herself for the walk down. She quickly passed through the brightness and glare of the city centre. Treading well known streets. Darting between shoppers and tourists. She avoided eye contact, fearing that each passer-by would somehow guess her destination.

Eventually she was outside the train station. She passed through the dark underpass that led the trains away from the city centre. An oppressive space at the best of times, made more unfriendly by the rumbles and groans of the locomotives above. Beth was relieved to emerge on to quieter streets beyond, even if this meant she was close to the Triangle.

A pause, to register where she was. Or maybe to change her mind and turn tail back into town.

The road she had stopped on was narrow. High stone walls ran along its sides. Cut into these were random openings, leading into old derelict yards and vacant car parks. It was a place a person could get all too easily lost in, by accident or design. She was close to her old beat now, could almost sense it.

It was not a pleasant feeling.

Adrenaline was making her take shorter breaths, she could feel her heart pound its urgent rhythm out inside her. Her will was saying no but her legs carried her along the street regardless. The same old route to her same old beat. Those familiar old walls rising like cliffs to both sides of her. The same old loneliness in an area where activity was more often hidden than celebrated.

'One, two, three four.'

She counted the lampposts. Just like she used to do in past days. Just around this corner now. Yes, there it was.

Beth paused on the junction of the street.

Her street.

It was all still there. Untouched by the sort of corporate development that was edging its way in around the perimeter of the Triangle. This place hadn't found favour with the big companies. Not yet, anyway.

There was the familiar patch of rough ground. How well she had known it. A dense barrier of brambles pushing up around it. The gap was still there though. Where you could sneak through and find a more private area. Do business, in the flattened grassed dip beyond.

Such a secluded spot. Cut off from the world. Time after time, doing business with a stranger, in a place cut off from the wider world. A private spot, too private. Beth shivered at the memory of all those potentially dangerous meetings in this place.

On the opposite side of the street was a flat, open scrubby field. Way off beyond that the grey outline of the motorway bypass filled the view. It stretched across the skyline. A grubby, angular beast.

She was lucky to have come away from here alive. There were times back then when she so very nearly didn't. Not that she wanted to remind herself of that. Especially not right here, right now.

'Nurse! Hey, Nurse Hooper!'

A voice behind her.

'What are you doing here?'

Leah was approaching. Her skinny frame tottering on unfeasibly high heels. A broad smile was plastered across her lips.

Skin deep, thought Beth.

The girl kept glancing back over her shoulder.

'It's not safe here Nurse, you need to watch your back.'

'Leah, please call me Beth. I came for you. Well, to find you. I was concerned about you, after our talk, I mean.'

A mixture of surprise and suspicion passed in waves across the girl's face. She shuffled from one foot to another, swaying a little on her stacked footwear. Beth watched the girl's teeth gnawing at the ragged skin at the edges of her mouth as Leah sucked in her lower lip.

'I'm alright, I can take care of myself. Anyways, it's not safe for a woman, here alone.'

'But you're here Leah, alone.'

Leah laughed harshly. 'I mean for a woman like you, not someone like me. I'm not alone anyway, which is why you need to go, now.'

Beth wanted to protest. She could see that Leah was becoming increasingly agitated. Her shuffling had become more pronounced and she rocked back and forth aggressively on her heels.

Beth held up her hands, inclining her head. 'Okay, okay. I'm going, but I'd really like it if you came to see me again at the clinic, please?'

Leah nodded vigorously, clearly keen to see the back of her. 'Yes, okay I will, but I've got to go and so should you. Bye.'

She tottered off quickly, to disappear back around the corner.

Beth waited a moment. Then carefully, she followed the girl and peered around the wall at the corner of the road. She could see into the side road without being seen from her vantage point.

The sight before her made the ground shift under her feet.

Was she having some kind of flashback? What she was seeing could not be real.

But no. There he was.

An all too familiar figure was hurrying Leah and another girl into a waiting car.

It couldn't be, could it?

The figure turned its head slightly, offering Beth a clearer view of their profile.

Fuck. It *was* him. Carl Jacobs, he was still here!

Her head was reeling. Of course he would be, why wouldn't he? This is what he did, who he was. He was all about the Triangle. She felt so dumb. Why hadn't she considered that she was likely to see him here?

God, what if he had spotted her?

The thought made her gag. She pushed her fist hard against her mouth to stifle any sound.

Even after all these years of staying away from him, from this place, Carl could still make her feel sick to her stomach. It would be so easy now to run and simply forget the whole idea. So tempting.

But she wanted to help Leah.

Even more so now she saw that Carl clearly had his claws in to her. Christ, it was like history repeating itself.

She'd been a similar age to Leah when she had been on the streets here, had walked in the girl's shoes. Like Leah and the other women down here she had climbed into the cars of strangers, night after night. Taken money from them in dark alleys, abandoned buildings and unknown homes. She had let men touch her, had touched them, had let them have sex with her for money, never knowing how each situation would end up. The risks and the fear had always been immense. But still she had carried on doing it, the need had been stronger.

Beth shuddered and hated herself for it.

Such a damn hypocrite. She must be, why else choose a job linked to the sex industry? If she thought she'd moved on she could think again. One big contradiction. To leave her old life behind only to bind herself back to it. Who did she think she was? Like some kind of born-again virgin preaching the word to others. Did she actually think she was now better than the women who came to the clinic?

She'd got out, supposedly changed her life but did that mean she was in a position to tell others what to do?

Just being here at the Triangle was having a significant effect on her self-worth. Beth felt like old insecurities pushing their way back up. They seemed to bubble into her throat like acidic vomit. What she wouldn't give for something to numb all of this right now.

Back then, Beth's life swam with drug use. It was true to say it was not like that for everyone. There were sex workers out there who were more in control, more protected, who had more choice in what they were doing. But equally there were plenty of women and men, then and now, suffering this stifling existence. Round and round on a circuit of sex for money. A pattern that was so hard to break.

For Beth, the way she had coped with the use of her body was drugs. A haze to distance the smells, the sight, the touch of the men.

Carl Jacobs had been only too happy to provide, even jokingly calling himself Doctor Carl. Talked about buying himself a white coat to wear when doling out the medication. The bringer of candy to get you through the good times and the bad. Doctor Carl was always ready to sedate. After all, it suited him to keep her numb and compliant.

Her addiction was deep by the time her father James, and sister, Cassie, had cottoned on to what was happening. But if it hadn't been for them, she would have been found dead, either by punter or needle. James and Cassie Hooper had quite literally saved her life.

She certainly hadn't thanked them for it at the time, but their intervention truly had made all the difference.

Beth had felt proud to have achieved such a change in her life, this job, this new role. It had taken some effort to get there. Five years of study of increasing intensity. Finally getting to taking her A-levels, much later than school. Then the culmination. Completing her nurse training.

Beth had started to work the wards at first but took every training opportunity to move her closer to her goal. She spent time voluntarily at the sexual health unit, making sure she got to know the staff and procedures. She wanted to work there so badly.

Right now, it seemed a little pompous and self-important, but she had wanted to put something back. Wanted to help the other sex workers out there in some way. So, when the job finally came up, she felt it had to be hers. There could be no one else better suited to it.

The effect of being back at her old beat was knocking all of that hard won positivity aside. She couldn't just let it go though, could she? Not after all that effort.

'Excuse me. Hi. You okay there?'

A slender young man had stepped out suddenly in front of her. Beth was taken aback. The light had started to fade and she was unsure just how long she had been standing there, stuck in her own head. These episodes of brief memory loss, blankness had been happening to her for years. She was unsurprised at the passing of time. However, the fact that it had occurred here, in this part of the city, was not a good thing and she had thought herself to be alone on the street.

She found an automatic expectation to hear those old questions from this young man. The sorts of things men used to ask her down here.

The young man had a pleasant friendly face. Quite good looking, Beth allowed herself to acknowledge, despite her discomfort. Her self-preservation kicked in. Always good to remember features, just in case. Green eyes beneath untidy dark curly hair. He was in need of a shave. More likely he was deliberately sporting a rash of stubble. Part of his carefully styled down-beat look.

He smiled at her. A warm smile, although she had been fooled before by good looks and seeming pleasantness.

'Yes, thank you.'

She tried to sound polite and dismissive at the same time, not wishing to be drawn into a conversation.

'It's just that I noticed that you had been standing here for a few minutes, just kinda staring into space. Wasn't sure if you were lost or something.'

Beth drew back a little from the young man. 'You were watching me?'

A warning tingle coursed down the back of her neck.

'Oh God no, well... I guess yes, but not in a creepy way. Oh dear, that sounds weird in itself, doesn't it?'

He wore a horrified look on his face.

'No, really I was just concerned about you. This is not the best of areas you know, not somewhere to linger if you don't know it well.'

'I know it well enough.'

'Oh? Right, sorry.'

'Yes, I used to work down here.'

She immediately regretted blurting such important information to a total stranger. Beth quickly tried to cover her tracks.

'Look I'm fine, really. Thank you for your concern but there's really no need.'

Turning to leave, Beth's urge was to get away from this place, and fast.

'Sure, no worries. I'm Josh by the way. Josh Simpson.'

'Okay.'

Beth had already set off but turned back, momentarily, to acknowledge him.

Josh took this as an opportunity. He quickly dived into the top pocket of his jacket. Beth flinched, but a simple business card was all he produced.

'Here,' he said proffering it towards her. 'This is me. Just so you know that I'm not some mad axe man or something.' He laughed weakly at his own joke.

Beth smiled a small tight twitch of her lips and took the card.

A journalist.

Huh! Now it makes sense. One to steer clear of then, she thought.

Best to be polite though. She still needed to leave here without any fuss.

'Thanks.'

She slipped the card into her bag and turned again to walk away.

He called after her.

'Nice to meet you.'

Yeah, I bet, she thought, simply raising one hand above her shoulder. Beth continued on her way.

CHAPTER 9

Harry had reviewed the CCTV footage a number of times. Each time he watched it he saw the car swing into the car park and then back out to drive around the corner, disappearing from the camera's view. It was Derek Foster's car; he was sure of that.

The footage was grainy due to the late hour and poor lighting in the area. Harry had frequently complained about it to his bosses. It had always fallen on deaf ears though.

The timer on the footage steadily ticked on. After a few minutes, a figure appeared. A female figure. Harry was pretty sure from their gait and the way they held themselves, that it was a woman. The indistinct footage showed a slender form wearing a short coat, or possibly a shirt dress. Harry was not a follower of fashion so could not be completely confident.

The figure's hair was evidently blonde, appearing as a light mass on the poor-quality images. It was long enough to swing and whip in the breeze as the figure appeared to look from side to side. Harry had reviewed the footage one more time. He felt sure of something. It was the posture and the manner of their movement that decided it for him.

It also made him anxious. It really did look like someone he knew. Someone he used to know. Not the usual street girls you got down the Triangle these days. No, someone else, from the past.

What to do?

Harry felt torn.

If it was *her* then... bloody hell. What had she got herself into?

A man had died though. He had to take action, was duty bound, wasn't he?

He sucked in the air through his teeth and made a quick lunge for the telephone. He tapped in the number and cleared his throat.

'Can I speak to DCI Bloom, please?'

CHAPTER 10

The clinic was quiet, for a change. Beth took the opportunity to make herself a cup of tea and catch up on some paperwork.

'Beth Hooper?'

Beth turned from the files she was updating.

'Yes?'

'DI Davidson. You'll remember me, I'm sure, and this is DCI Bloom.'

The female officer and her colleague advanced into the surgery.

'We would like to talk to you about your movements over the last few days.'

Even though it had only been Davidson that had visited her previously, Beth recognised both officers. She and DCI Peter Bloom had most definitely met before. She momentarily locked eyes with the senior officer.

Unhappy to see the police again in her clinic room, she nodded curtly and indicated towards a nearby chair. Davidson took the offered seat leaving Bloom to hang back behind his junior officer. He looked sullen.

Same old Bloom, Beth thought.

'Okay, what's this about then?'

Despite the presence of the more senior officer, DI Davidson took the lead. 'Can you tell us your whereabouts this week please, Nurse Hooper?'

'What, the whole week? Every day, every minute of the day? That's a bit much for anyone to remember, don't you think?'

She knew she sounded awkward, petulant even. She couldn't resist it. The presence of the police always had that effect on her.

Plus, there were gaps in her memory. It had been that way for years. Little fuzzy patches where she couldn't quite grasp hold of a memory. She had been pretty sure it was normal, like that for everyone. Most people forgot the passing of their journey to and from work, or what they had said to someone after a few pints at the pub. But Beth forgot conversations. She couldn't remember visiting some places or who she was with. That wasn't right. She knew it and had mentioned it to a colleague once, hoping for reassurance that this was all perfectly usual. When she had explained how there were times, particularly late in the evening, when she would mentally shut down before coming back to herself, like awakening from an unremembered dream, the other nurse had looked concerned. She had patted Beth's arm and suggested she seek expert guidance with the problem.

Beth had yet to heed that advice.

Davidson appeared to be ignorant of Beth's attitude, or so used to coming up against this type of resistance that it washed off her. She continued.

'Yes, both daytime and the nights please.'

'Well, this does feel sort of unnecessarily intrusive, but if you must know I have been here at the clinic all week. Day time I mean. Then in the evenings I have visited my father over in the main hospital, he is on a ward there, and then I've gone home. Alone.'

'And stayed at your own home each night, until morning?'

'Yes.'

'Can anyone vouch for you being at your flat each evening, Miss Hooper?'

Beth vaguely wondered how they knew she lived in a flat, but then they were the police. It wouldn't have been too hard for them to find out in their background check of her.

'I live alone so no, although some of my neighbours may have seen me coming in after work and leaving in the mornings.'

There was a moment of silence as Davidson scribbled down notes in her pad. Beth looked over at Bloom. He was making a concerted effort to avoid any eye contact, busily interrogating the pattern in the floor tiles.

The whole situation was deeply uncomfortable. Beth felt a desperate urge to break the oppression of the moment.

'Look what is this about? If you tell me, maybe I can –'

Davidson raised one hand, the palm facing Beth to interrupt her. The pencil the officer had been writing with was sticking forward between two fingers. Was the officer about to jab it into her face? She quickly dismissed the thought as Davidson asked again.

'So, no-one can say for definite that they saw you each evening of this week, after you left the hospital ward where your father currently is. Is that correct?'

'Well yes, I guess so, but –'

Davidson interrupted once more, this time seeming to change tack.

'When we last spoke you advised me that you had frequented the Triangle in the past. Tell me, do you ever find the need to visit the Triangle, these days I mean, Miss Hooper?'

Beth was taken aback. Had they seen her down there looking for Leah? No... what they were asking was just about the evenings and night-time, wasn't it? Isn't that when the local news reports were saying that those men had been found dead in their cars? Not during the day.

She may be feeling a tad paranoid, but surely they didn't think she had something to do with those men dying? When Davidson had visited her before she had intimated that there might have been foul play. Maybe they did actually think she was a suspect in this! How the hell had this happened?

Should she be honest or cautious with them? Beth chose the latter.

'Err, generally no but occasionally for my work.'

'Really? When we last spoke you told me you hadn't been down there in years and that you never did outreach work. So, would you like to explain why now you are telling us something different and in what way this is connected to your work?'

'Well yes, I did say that I don't do outreach work and that is the truth. It isn't part of my job. But on the odd occasion, if I'm really concerned about a particular patient and I know they work down there, then I might go down and check on them.'

'But that's not really part of your job, is that what you are saying?'

'That's right. It isn't, not strictly. But I guess if you care about people and do a caring job, you can't always switch off when your patients' situations affect you.'

'I see, but isn't there an issue of protocol in that Nurse Hooper? Surely if it's not part of your role then your employer would find that of considerable concern?'

Annoyingly, Beth knew the police officer was right about that. A clipped 'Yes' was as much as she could muster in response.

Davidson nodded, clearly happy to have hit the mark. She glanced momentarily at her colleague but Bloom remained silent.

'I see, and despite what you previously told me, were you in fact down in the Triangle area this week, Miss Hooper, seeing one of the patients?'

'Yes, I was. It was yesterday. Honestly, it was the first time I've been down there in years. I went down after work so it would have been about 5.00pm, maybe 5.30pm or thereabouts. I didn't stay long either. Once I had spoken to the person I wanted see, I left. Believe me, I had no interest in hanging around down there.'

'And then after visiting the area you went where exactly?'

'Well, home, of course.'

'So, are you saying you only visited the Triangle once in recent weeks and that was during early evening hours and that you have not visited the area in the late evening or during the night at all over the last few weeks, is that correct Nurse Hooper?'

Davidson tapped out a rhythm with her pencil down her notepad as she spoke.

'I've already told you; I was at home each and every evening. I stayed home all night and didn't leave my flat until the following morning.'

Bloom finally spoke. 'But you do know the Triangle well, don't you, Beth? You've spent time down there. Why did you suggest to DI Davidson otherwise?'

Beth grimaced at the senior officer. Why did he have to step in now when she thought she had said enough to make them leave her alone?

'Well yes, but it was a long time ago, when I was a teenager. Yeah, back then I did hang out down there. But like I say, that was years ago. I already said that to her.'

She gestured towards Davidson.

'Yes, but you also said previously that you hadn't been recently and now we find out you have. You can see why that would concern us, can't you Beth?'

'Well yes, I guess so, but I never meant to deliberately mislead you–'

'Okay, Nurse Hooper, thank you for your time.'

Beth noted Bloom's use of formality.

'We may need to talk to you again so please do not leave the city if you can avoid doing so or at the very least inform us immediately if you do, understood?'

'Yes, I understand.'

Bloom and Davidson departed. Beth felt oddly emptied, flattened by their carefully phrased yet accusatory words. Maybe it was the mention from Bloom of her former days down at The Triangle, maybe the whole damn mess her life had been back then was finally going to hit home.

When she had got clean and sorted her life out, with the help of Dad and Cassie, she had felt like she could take on any challenge, win them all, or at least equal them. She had been so positive. The realities of linking her old life to her new had not even occurred to her.

Potential murders, what the hell! And that the police thought she was actually involved. This was madness.

She had genuinely, if a little naively, thought it would be easy to do this job. Thought she was equipped to handle it. Promised herself she would keep a professional distance between herself and the beat.

But was she distanced from it, really? Beth couldn't help but question herself about her motives now. She needed to face it; the fact was she had deliberately sought out a role that tethered her to that existence.

Hadn't her reasoning been good? She wanted to right some wrongs somehow. Self aggrandising as that sounded right now, surely that wasn't a bad thing?

The conflicts of it all swamped her. When she had been on the streets, she had been a mess, spiralling downward in her own misery. She knew even then she wasn't a bad person, just someone who had wandered into a bad situation.

Still, leaving it all behind - the money and drugs, even Carl - had been so difficult. Despite the support and help of Dad and Cas the temptation to return to the Triangle had been immense and it had taken months, years really, for that need to calm enough to become manageable.

It didn't matter that she knew it was all so self-destructive. It didn't matter what her father or others had said about the way she had been manipulated. There was still a piece of her that felt she must have deserved it all. Penance for being so stupid. Only a stupid girl would get into that sort of mess, right? Only an idiot girl would let Carl into her life, let him control her, wouldn't she? She had been so deep into it all that her sense of self-worth just hadn't existed anymore. Back then, even she had seen herself as a commodity.

It was all too much. The room seemed to suddenly press in close around her. She needed space, open sky, to breathe. Telling the reception staff that she was going on her break, she headed out to get some air.

Walking in a daze. Deep in thought. Just one foot plodding rhythmically in front of the other. Plodding, blind to what was around her, she passed silently along the well-known street. Finally, she found herself standing once more on her old corner in the Triangle.

'Fuck, my head! What the hell am I doing to myself, coming here again?'

She scanned the all too familiar road. It was just after lunchtime, so the area was quiet. Too early for most of the girls to be out, although she imagined there must be a few who'd done some business already.

Being here, on her patch, in this place, it was as if a different person had lived that life. She had naively thought it would be so easy to remove herself from it now, in her fresh, clean flat, or with her new workmates chatting and sharing a laugh down at the pub after work. There she had imagined she would be the happy confident Beth. The one who had her act together, who knew who she was. The one whose life had panned out right.

She would have gone to university, working in a hospital (at least she had achieved *that* goal). Maybe gotten married, maybe bought her own house. At least lived with a partner and had a family. All this and a successful career. She had been meant to have it all. She was still that little girl inside. Those childhood dreams were a million miles away from this place though, and how life had been here.

Here she had been forced to learn to be different, to be resourceful, pliable, be astute and be selfish. You had to be, to survive.

The first man, the very first one, was still with her. She remembered. She didn't want to, pretended not to, but she remembered them all. They could blur into a hazy mess of drug-coated encounters, all flesh and drowsily heard instructions. But if she allowed herself to focus, she knew they were all distinguishable.

It was best not to. Too hard to deal with. It was bad enough when the more forceful memories pushed their way up. None of them were wanted, they should all be buried, not picked at like some oozing open sore.

This was why she wanted to help the other women down there. She was in no position to judge them and if they wanted to, HAD to carry on working the Triangle, then the least she could do was try to make them a little safer, a little more protected. It was a good thing, not just something to salve her conscience.

But why were the police intimating she was in some way connected to the deaths of those punters? Why now after all these years away from the beat? Why would they think she would do such a thing and why do it now when she had gotten herself into a much better place in life?

'Alright there, love? Long time no see.'

Harry.

Beth was delighted and relieved to see an old friend. Harry had been a reliable source of support many times when she had worked the beat. She reached out to briefly embrace him, noting that he had put on weight since she had last seen him.

'Harry, what a welcome surprise. So lovely to see you. I didn't know if you would still be working down here. I actually thought you might have retired.'

Harry chuckled. 'There's life in the old dog yet, love. Not quite ready for the pipe and slippers, you know. Plus, I'd only be under Mrs Wood's feet, wouldn't I, and then she'd be finding me all sorts of little jobs to do around the house.'

Beth laughed, enjoying the relaxed moment. 'Yes, I guess she would.'

'You know me Beth love, I would get bored at home, wouldn't I? I'm a people person. I need to be out and about. I enjoy the buzz of it all down here and they still need me here, you know.'

She nodded wondering whether the management of the industrial estate really did value him. It would be nice to think they did, she certainly always had.

'Well now love, what brings you down here, eh? Thought we'd not see you again. Not that it isn't a pleasure to see you, of course.'

Always had a polite charm about him, Harry. Something of an old school gentleman. He had always treated her and the other girls with the utmost respect.

'Thank you, Harry. I'm working up at the sexual health clinic these days, you know... as a nurse. Got myself qualified, the lot.'

Harry beamed. 'Well, well, well! That is fantastic love. I'm so pleased for you. It's not often we get to hear a good luck story down here. Well done Beth, I'm dead happy to hear that you've done so well for yourself.'

Beth grinned back. She allowed herself to enjoy their shared pride in her achievements.

'Yes, I have definitely changed direction in my life, but I've not forgotten my past, you know. Nor the people down here, especially the girls. Which is why I'm working at the clinic now. I wanted to be in a position where I could help other girls who found themselves in the sort of life that I used to lead, you know?'

Harry nodded. 'Very commendable it is too, love. Is that why you are down here then? Is it part of your job, coming down to do visits to the girls then?'

'Not exactly, Harry. To be honest, I have tried to steer clear of the beat. I'm very much clinic-based really. I find it more manageable that way.'

Harry smiled understandingly.

'It's just this one girl, though. Well, she's so young, vulnerable like. You know what I mean?'

'Yes, love. They seem to get younger each time I come out to patrol, or maybe it's that I'm getting older.'

Beth smiled and patted Harry's arm.

'Yeah, I've just had a feeling about this one girl who came into the centre and it wouldn't leave me. It kept nagging at me, so I just seemed to have ended up down here.'

'Oh right, so this is the first time you've been down the Triangle lately then?'

Beth wondered about the slight tone of surprise in Harry's voice. 'Yeah, it's been literally years since I've been here.'

Oh right, very good.'

Harry seemed quite pleased, almost relieved by her answer.

'Yes, as I said, I have been at pains to avoid the place so far. If it wasn't for this one girl coming in, well, I'm pretty sure I would not be standing here right now talking to you.'

Harry stroked his chin a little and nodded again. 'And this girl, was she the one you were talking to the other day? Around the corner, I mean.'

'You saw us?'

'Yes, on the CCTV, when I was looking back through some footage. Don't worry love, I wasn't being a voyeur or anything. It's part of my job on security to spool back through footage sometimes if there's been any dodgy activity around the units. It's not really part of the boss's site but you can see that street quite clearly on the edge of the view from one of our cameras.'

'Of course not, Harry. It's okay. I know you are one of the good guys. But yeah, that was her.'

'Ah okay, I think her name is Leah, am I right?'

Beth nodded.

'Skinny little thing. Looks like she need a few good meals.'

'You're not wrong there Harry, although my main concern is the company she is keeping. She's with Carl.'

'What, you mean Carl Jacobs?'

Beth nodded

Harry sucked in a breath between clenched teeth.

'Well, that's not good. That's not good at all.'

'I know. Look, Harry... could you do me a massive favour? Could you keep an eye on Leah for me a bit? I can't be down here much, I just don't feel it would be good for me to be here, but I can't just leave Leah in the hands of that monster.'

'Far too polite a name for him in my view, but of course I will love. Let's exchange phone numbers so I can let you know if I see anything that I think you need to be worried about.'

'Thank you so much Harry, I will try to come back down occasionally, but really I would like to try to get her away from here and from *him*. I know it's ultimately up to her, but really, I don't think being down here is in any way good for a kid like her. And Carl, well he isn't good for *anyone* to hang around with.'

'I understand, Beth. Look, here's my phone number. You can rely on me, love.'

Once Beth had keyed their numbers into their respective phones, Harry set off back to his broom cupboard office. He'd felt a wash of relief when Beth had said she hadn't been down to the area in a few years. Yet a small twinge of doubt and confusion remained. After all, there was that CCTV footage he had seen.

But no, he repressed it. He just could not imagine that a lovely girl like Beth could be caught up in murder. He didn't want to it to be possible. Harry had such mixed feelings about making that phone call to the police about the blonde figure he had seen. Couldn't have lived with himself if that had been a piece of key evidence that would have helped the police find the killer though.

Just think if more men die because you don't speak up, he had told himself at the time. But still, there were a few people down the Triangle that would give him a hard time if they found out what he had done. A grass. That's what they would see him as. His name, the trust and reputation he had built up over the years, all that would be mud.

Plus, there was Beth. He genuinely cared for the girl, always had since he had first encountered her. That gangly, wide-eyed kid, dressed up like she was in her mother's high heels and lipstick. His paternal instinct had kicked in immediately. He was delighted to have seen her again and the fact that she was clearly doing so well for herself had given him a real boost.

Beth was comforted by the rekindling of their close bond. Reassured by the fact that an old friendly face was still keeping an eye on the girls. Even if that was as far as it went with Harry. He had never been one to physically step in when there had been trouble, and at his advanced age nor would she want him to do so now. Despite this, she was pretty sure that on those occasions back in those past days, when the police had turned up, he'd probably been the one that had made the call.

Funny how so much of this place was still so set in time. Other parts of the city had seen massive changes, buildings knocked down, new shiny tower blocks put up in their place. The city positively hummed with the energy of so many people, like worker ants scurrying this way and that to their offices, gathering goods from all the shiny new shopping centres that seemed to have sprouted up.

The heart of the area remained just as it had been when she had spent all of her nights here. The same tired old buildings, some now propped up with scaffolding, bearing 'danger: do not enter' notices. She bet some of the current girls down there did chance it in them. Punters always wanted somewhere quiet so what better place than these derelict edifices of brick and stone, silent with only their memories etched into the crumbling walls.

The beat, her beat, may have become a little more overgrown than she remembered, but really it was just the same. It was in some ways the most shocking part of it for Beth. Was her new life a dream? Being there again, it kind of felt like it. As if she'd never left.

She looked down at herself. Sensible shoes, tights and the nurse's uniform showing under her trench coat.

A laugh forced itself from her tightened throat.

Don't be so daft! she thought. *Of course, your new life is real. All this is just a memory, this is a dream now, or a nightmare, more like.*

Wrenching herself free from these thoughts she started to walk back up to the clinic. As she set off, Leah strolled casually around the corner towards her.

'Hiya.'

'Leah hi, how are you? Are you on your own?'

Leah was toying with her mobile phone. 'I'm fine, me. Couldn't be better. It's all good.'

Beth frowned not quite believing the girl's upbeat words.

'Anyway, only came over to say hello, can't stop, got stuff to do, I'm literally so busy today.'

Leah gazed off into the distance then back down at her phone.

Beth saw a possibility. 'Well, good to see you anyway. How would you feel about me giving you my phone number? For if you need a chat anytime the clinic isn't open?'

The girl shrugged. 'Yeah okay, suppose so, it's up to you really, yeah I guess if you want to–'

Leah handed her the phone and Beth deftly tapped in her number and hit save. Grabbing the mobile back from Beth the young girl said simply, 'Gotta go.'

She spun on her heels and set off away from Beth.

'Bye then, Leah,' Beth called after her. 'Don't forget to call or message if you need a chat or anything.'

Leah appeared not to have heard, but then Beth's phone chirped the arrival of a new message.

It was Leah, an address, an invitation.

Beth quickly texted back her acceptance, relieved and pleased that she had evidently made a breakthrough with the girl. Pocketing her phone, she set off back into the City.

CHAPTER 11

Beth's next appointment was a no show. She made her way to reception to find out if there was a problem.

Davidson and Bloom rose in unison, seemingly happy to free themselves from the uncomfortable perch of the plastic clinic chairs.

'Hello Beth, could we have word please?' said Bloom.

Beth rolled her eyes. It was annoying to see them again and so soon.

She called out to the receptionist, 'Any sign of my next appointment, Lucy?'

Lucy shook her head. 'Apologies Beth, it's been so full-on on the desk here today I hadn't had chance to tell you. They rang to cancel.'

People not turning up wasn't uncommon. Right now, it was irritating. Beth had no obvious excuse for not seeing the police officers. Nor could she think of anything else to put them off. Reluctantly, she turned to Davidson and Bloom.

'Do I have choice? Well, I guess it looks like I have a couple of minutes free now then. Come through, please.'

The detectives followed Beth back into the privacy of the consultation room. Bloom firmly closed the door.

'Thank you,' he started. 'This shouldn't take too long. We just want you to go over your movements again for the last few days, please.'

Beth's temper spiked. This was so frustrating. Surely, they had gone through all of this the last time they had turned up unannounced? But no. Here they were again. Asking her the same old questions. She felt persecuted. When would this end?

'Really, haven't I already told you that? I'm pretty sure I have said all I can. I don't know what else to tell you.'

Davidson interjected.

'Well maybe something will have sparked a memory for you since then. It might only be a small detail, but it could be something important to us.'

'I really don't see how. Like I said before, I haven't been down the Triangle for years up until this last week and then I only went because I was worried about a patient. As I told you before, DI Davidson, it was definitely the end of the working day, so early evening and I didn't stay down there for very long.'

'So you said you just met this young woman 'Leah' down there. How come you were also recently seen talking to a security guard, Harry Woods? You spoke to him in the same vicinity, isn't that right? Anything else you would like to tell us about?'

Beth didn't recall mentioning Harry to the DI the last time they had met. After all, she had only seen him after the police had paid her their visit. She was also sure that she had not mentioned Leah by name.

Had they been following her? Monitoring her movements? Davidson's manner, and this repeated harassment they seemed intent on engaging in, was starting to freak Beth out. She did her best to reply calmly.

'No. I did not meet anyone else down there. Obviously, I did see other people walking about. Surely you would expect that? Okay, let me be totally frank here... I *did* catch a glimpse of Carl Jacobs, but that's all it was, just a glance, from a distance.' Beth could have bitten her own tongue off for mentioning Carl.

'Carl Jacobs and Harry Wood? You certainly seemed to have been in a chatty mood when you returned the Triangle. Why didn't' you mention this the last time we spoke?'

'I didn't think it was important.'

'I see. Well, Nurse Hooper, I would say failing to advise us of two men who frequent the area is rather important, wouldn't you? As we have tried to stress, any piece of information, no matter how small you may consider it to be, could be important to us.'

'Harry does not frequent the area, as you put it. But yes, he was there. And as for Carl, I really only saw him from down the street. I didn't speak to him, at all. It honestly was just for a moment.'

'You're sure about that?'

'Of course I'm bloody sure.'

Bloom interjected. 'Alright Beth, no need to get upset, we are only asking you a few questions.'

She was angry, but with a deep breath in, Beth nodded her confirmation.

Davidson glanced over at Bloom then continued. 'So you say that you didn't go down to the Triangle with the intention of meeting with Carl Jacobs, is that correct?'

'Absolutely not. Look, I'm not a bloody masochist you know. Why would I want to get involved with him again? He is the last person I would want to see.'

DI Davidson looked up, intrigued. 'I understand you had a relationship with him some years ago, is that right?'

'You evidently know that it is, but that doesn't mean I want to see him again. Or that I would wish to go back and spend time down in that area. I am not involved with Carl Jacobs now, or with what happened to those punters.'

Bloom and Davidson exchanged looks.

'I don't recall saying you had been involved with the men that were found down there. Interesting that you would use the word 'punters' to describe them though.'

Beth was furious with herself. She really would end up saying too much. The way this was playing out, if they hadn't thought she was involved before, she bet damn sure that they thought it now.

'No but...'

'"But" suggests that there might be something you want to tell us. Is that the case, Beth?'

'No! Absolutely not. I am in no way involved with anything going on down there. I may work in sexual health but seriously, my life does not revolve around hanging out down at the Triangle. What possible reason could I have for hurting those men? I didn't even know them through the clinic. Seriously, they were nothing to me.'

'But you did just call them punters and isn't it true to say that you have no alibis for the times the men in question died? Isn't that the case?'

Beth felt increasingly flustered by the questioning. 'Well, I guess it's a term I've picked up from the clinic. The women do speak quite frankly to us at times and yes, as I stated before I was alone in my flat at the times you said those men died. You know, I did say pretty much all of this the last time we spoke. That hasn't changed and I am sure that there are thousands of people across the city without alibis for those times when you say the men were attacked. I just don't understand why you have singled me out as someone who could possibly be involved.'

'Expect you forgot to mention your little sighting of Carl Jacobs last time.'

'Yeah, and I've just explained that to you.'

Davidson snapped her notebook shut. The two detectives traded another glance and Bloom nodded to his colleague.

'Okay then Beth, thanks for your time today,' said Davidson.

'What, that's it then?'

'Yes, for now. We may want to speak to you again but for the time being that's it. We will see ourselves out and thanks.'

Trembling. Her heart pounding an uncomfortable rhythm inside her. How come they could always do this to her? She'd done nothing wrong, but she guessed old behaviour had a habit of resurfacing. She realised her hands were clawed into fists and the room felt hot and confining. She moved to the open window to gulp in some fresher air, thankful for a light breeze blowing in.

Out in the carpark, Bloom and Davidson were visible. They were standing with a third person. A man. He looked vaguely familiar to Beth. Where had she seen him before? She watched the trio waving gestures and mouthing words to each other, but they were too far away to allow her to hear any of their conversation.

Then it clicked. Josh, the journalist. She had taken his card. She turned to reach under her desk and rifle through her handbag. There was the card and that was definitely him. Josh Simpson.

She hunched into the side of the window recess, trying her best to be invisible, and looked back out at the three figures. They clearly knew each other well. There seemed to be a relaxed air between them. She watched as they finally parted, waving their goodbyes to each other like long-time friends.

Josh now appeared to be heading towards the clinic.

That's all I need, thought Beth.

She returned to her desk and checked her appointments calendar. Annoyingly, after her absentee's appointment, there wasn't anyone else booked in to see her for another hour. Unless she had a walk-in patient appear then she would struggle to avoid having to speak to the journalist.

The phone on her desk chirped. It was Lucy at reception telling her that Josh Simpson was here, asking to speak to her.

Damn it, she thought. Although... maybe if she spoke to him now, she could stop him coming back to pester her for a story. It wasn't the first time the clinic had had the press pushing them for details on particular patients. Her boss Jenny had taken pains to warn her that this could happen from time to time when the local paper was looking to create some sleazy story.

She sighed and said into the handset, 'Okay Lucy, send him through but let him know I only have about ten minutes free. I don't want him thinking he can take up a slot if someone does a walk-in.'

A few moments later there was a light rapping on the room door.

'Come in,' Beth called, remaining seated at her desk.

'Hello Nurse.' Josh Simpson entered smiling broadly.

'Good to see you again.' Beth's smile was thinner. She inclined her head towards the seat to the opposite side of her desk.

'What can I do for you, Mr Simpson?'

'Josh. Please call me Josh.'

'Okay, Josh, what can I help you with? Do you have any symptoms that you would like us to look at for you?'

Beth knew that he was unlikely to be here for any treatment but she couldn't resist the opportunity to toy with him a little.

'Err, no. Thanks, but no. I'm fine on that score. No, it was a bit of background information I was hoping for really.'

'Well, I'm sure you know that the dealings of the clinic are confidential.'

'Yes of course, and I would never expect you to divulge an individual's personal details, it's just that I wondered if there had been anything particularly unusual occurring lately? Without giving too much away, are you able to tell me if there have been any unexpected people visiting the clinic lately?'

'As I've just said, we cannot give out that kind of information plus I don't understand what you mean by unexpected people. We have an extremely diverse cross section of society visiting us here. No one is what you could call *unexpected* in my view, but everyone is an individual. I am really struggling to understand just what it is you are getting at, Mr Simpson.'

'My apologies Nurse Hooper, and like I said, it's Josh, please. I certainly don't mean to cause offence and I'm sure you get a lot more people than the usual street-walker types, but it's just whether you have had a rise in older people coming in that I am interested in.'

Beth raised one eyebrow, regarding him coolly.

'You make a rather large assumption about the supposed type of women who enter into sex work by your use of words there, Mr Simpson. Seems to me you have just shown yourself to be somewhat narrow-minded if you have bought into some kind of clichéd view that only one type of person does sex work.'

She was pleased to see that her words had hit the mark. Josh Simpson had turned a deep shade of crimson. He stuttered slightly in his response.

'No, no not at all.' He let out a nervous laugh. 'I guess it's just that we've all seen films like *Pretty Woman* after all.'

Beth's demeanour must have shown she did not share in the weak joke. After a pause she spoke again; her tone was even, measured.

'There, Mr Simpson... you have again fallen into the trap of the stereotype and yes, I know you were attempting to be humorous, but believe me... we have heard it all before here and it doesn't sound any less uneducated coming from the mouth of a journalist. So, let me enlighten you, as it does seem that you are in need of a broader view on the subject.'

'Yes, sorry, poor choice of reference material in that film. At least I didn't mention the Happy Hooker though, eh.'

She ignored him and continued. 'The facts are that people from all walks of life enter into sex work. It's not just a matter of the person having had a traumatic or difficult upbringing. There are people involved in this type of work who are from very stable backgrounds as well. There is no one-size-fits-all type of personality involved here, Mr Simpson. People end up doing this sort of work for lots of different reasons and stay doing it often for other reasons. Also, once you are involved in that lifestyle it's not an easy one to break away from, not without help in most cases. Allowing your body to be used by other people in that way is not an easy choice for the majority of the women and men involved in sex work, but for some people it becomes the only choice.'

Josh had looked pained. He leant forward in his chair; his hands held palm to palm.

'Look, I'm really sorry, I think we got off on the wrong foot here. I need to assure you that I am very much not the person you think I am and those are not my views. I apologise wholeheartedly. I realise my attitude may have come across as being not terribly serious about the matter and that again was not my intention.'

Beth started to wonder if she had been a little hard on him. She was always on the defensive first with men, even these days.

'I'll be honest with you Nurse Hooper, the reasons I wanted to speak to you, wanted some help on this... I think there is something happening down the Triangle, to men visiting sex workers, I mean.'

After the visits by the police, it didn't take any effort for Beth to work out what he was getting at. Josh continued. 'So yes, as you may have surmised, I am looking to write a story about this. But I would appreciate it if you would allow me a moment to explain my motives to you?'

She was intrigued and nodded her agreement.

'Thank you. Okay, where to begin... okay, yes well, I think I will just tell you it straight. When I was in Uni, I lived in halls of residence and, of course, you make friends with the people on your floor, start hanging out, sussing everyone out.

'Anyway, there was this one girl, a bit different than the rest of us. She kind of had a mysterious air about her. She was out most evenings but not at the student union or in any of the pubs we frequented. I was intrigued by her, wanted to understand what was going on with her. So, I made an effort to befriend her. To cut a long story short, we got close, as friends, and she confided in me that she worked the beat.'

'I see, go on, please.'

'I'm kind of ashamed to say that having her as a friend ended up being some sort of cool badge of honour. We were all so desperate to be special, different, back then and there she was, a true individual leading a very different life to us, and all to pay for her studies. She seemed sophisticated, in a way. Shows how foolish we all were, huh? It all came to a head one night when I found her in the common room collapsed and bleeding. She had been badly beaten by a client and had managed to make her way back to the halls.'

A spasm cramped Beth's belly.

'Thankfully, the University services stepped in to help her at that point and it's a good job too. I certainly didn't have a clue what to do for her. The truth is I felt really guilty about that for years. Not trying to stop her doing it, I mean. Thinking it was cool, and edgy to have a friend in the sex industry. I was such an idiot.'

His head dropped a little. Beth automatically reached across the desk to place a comforting hand on his arm.

'No, just young and immature I imagine,' Beth said kindly, 'at least you told someone who could help her.'

'Yeah, but it had to get to the point of her getting seriously hurt before I did. That's the thing that stays with me and whenever anything comes up about the sex industry, or the Triangle, I always ask my editor if I can have the piece. I want to try to make sure that at least my newspaper reports on it with honesty and integrity.'

Beth wondered if she had been too hasty in her judgement of him. 'Okay maybe I was a little strong in my response to you too. It's just that I get annoyed by the way sex workers are treated as lesser members of society. Those that do it are still people. Still human beings. They are someone's daughter, wife, son, sister, brother and they have the same feelings, needs and wants as anyone else does. I just think they deserve more understanding and respect than they are currently afforded.'

Josh shuffled further forward on his seat and vigorously nodded. 'I totally agree, believe me... my motives are to report the truth here and to give a fair balance to everyone.'

'Fine, I'm glad we understand each other better now, but I still can't tell you any details.'

'I know and that's fine. I understand but I am pleased we have had chance to talk like this.'

'As am I.'

Josh rose to leave, but turned back for to look at her. 'Maybe we could talk again some time?'

'Yes, maybe we could.'

A final grin from Josh sealed the moment, then he was gone. She picked up his business card and slowly rotated it between her fingers. Maybe it wouldn't be such a bad thing if she did see him again, she thought before pushing the card into the top drawer of the desk.

CHAPTER 12

Leah lived in a large, converted terrace house. It was a rundown part of the city, close to the Triangle. A large advertisement board in the garden emboldened with words 'luxury studio apartments for rent' and showed computer generated images of aspirational designer living. In truth, the flats had been created on the cheap. Studio apartments made from single rooms in what had originally been a large single Victorian dwelling.

Inside the building, Leah let Beth into her flat. The so-called studio apartment was tiny. It housed little more than a bed, a two-seater sofa, a small wooden table, and a kitchenette. A cramped shower room was built awkwardly across one corner of the room.

Luxury studio apartment? thought Beth. *I guess it's a roof over her head, but they've a funny idea about what constitutes luxury. When I left home, these sorts of places were considered to be the lower end of the market and they don't appear to have improved much since those days. I suppose at least she has her own shower room and doesn't have to suffer the indignity of a bathroom in a shared house, like I had to.*

She let her gaze wander, taking in the meagre room. Leah had tried to make it homely by hanging posters and ethnic printed throws on the walls. A few ornaments had been arranged in a line at the back edge of the small table. One of the wall hangings had sagged. Beth could see the black mottled circles of mould in the gap. She wondered how far the damp was spreading itself along the covered walls and shuddered to think of Leah sleeping in here.

The sofa was piled high with a tangled mess of clothing. Beth seated herself on the end of the bed.

'Leah, you don't have to live like this you know'.

Leah raised her eyebrows. 'Oh yeah, I know. This is just my holiday home like. I move back into my mansion next week.'

'No, seriously Leah, there is help out there, I want to help you, if you'll let me.'

'Like what? What do you think you can actually do? It's not like the Council waiting list is just gonna disappear and they are going to offer me a new home, is it? I'm pretty sure you're not gonna offer me one either, eh. Bet you live in a lovely place, in a good area. Fancy a lodger? No, didn't think so.'

'But Leah –'

'Look Beth, seriously, just leave it, you don't know me well enough, or my life. Please, just leave it. I'm fine really. It's all good.'

'Leah, I –'

Beth was interrupted this time by the flat door opening.

'Well, well, well, what an unexpected pleasure!'

Carl Jacobs stood before them both, his large frame filling the open doorway.

'Well, I'll be damned. Beth! And there was me thinking you has the idea that you were too good for the likes of us these days. Good to see you girl.'

Beth's stomach flipped. She would have liked nothing better than to get up, push him out of the way and run as fast as she could, without looking back.

Leah scurried around the tiny flat

'Hiya, Carl. You alright? Want a coffee, Carl? Here sit down.'

She hurriedly gathered up the tangled limbs of the pile of T-shirts and leggings from the small sofa, dumping them in a twisted heap on the floor.

Carl ignored her and moved to position himself seated on the bed, next to Beth.

'Don't I even get a hello then, girl?'

'Hello Carl.'

'That's a bit more like it, how's about a hug then as well?'

Beth visibly blanched. Carl laughed. She had forgotten quite how mockingly cruel his laugh could sound.

'Only kidding girl, I know you think you're better than the likes of us now, with your qualifications and your new job. Not one of us anymore, are you?'

Beth said nothing and looked down. From the corner of her eye, she could see that Carl was watching her, a smirk playing on his lips.

'I knew it was you when I saw you in the hospital car park. Never forget a face do I, or a body for that matter.'

Beth cringed at his crudity. Carl appeared to be revelling in her discomfort. Then the sudden shock of realising that he knew where she worked. Why wouldn't he have seen her? She felt quite a fool. If she'd thought about it, she would have realised that it was Carl who had accompanied Leah to the clinic.

'Oh really? Well, I didn't see you.'

Carl flashed her that smile again. She felt sure that he would have liked nothing better than to have devoured her, right there and then.

'Ha, yeah international man of mystery, ain't I.'

Beth smiled weakly.

Leah hovered next to the kitchenette, fidgeting and tapping her feet. She watched them both intently.

'So, you two know each other, right?'

Carl barked another laugh, cocking his head sharply with an audible snap. He looked sideways at Beth. 'Oh yeah, Beth and I are old pals ain't we? Go way, way back. She was one of my best, weren't you girl?'

The girl looked shocked and hurt, Beth was overcome with guilt for not confiding in her. She hoped the young woman could read the apology in her eyes.

'You? You worked the beat? Why didn't you tell me? Fuck Beth, why did you keep that from me? I thought we were becoming mates.'

'We were Leah, we are. Look I'm really sorry, it didn't seem important at the time and it was such a long time ago, another lifetime.'

'Not fucking important? You're talking about what IS my life!'

'You're right Leah, it is important, you're important. I totally didn't mean it that way. I have total respect for you. Please believe me. That came out all wrong. I'm sorry, please, forgive me.'

Carl had been sitting back obviously enjoying the exchange between the two women. He now interjected.

'Hey! It's a damn good life that I give you Leah, and don't you fucking forget it, and you had no cause to fucking complain back in the day, Beth.'

'Are you fucking serious, Carl?' Beth was incredulous at the brazen attitude of the man. She had quite forgotten the enormity of his ego.

'Yeah, course I'm fucking serious. If it wasn't for me, Leah wouldn't be half as well looked after.'

Beth looked up at the girl. She didn't have the look of a cared for person. Knowing Carl, it would be more like control than care. Leah flinched under her gaze. A tired, skinny girl. Broken. That's how she looked to Beth.

Carl oblivious, continued. 'Hell, you're back, ain't ya Beth. So, it can't have been all bad.'

'I am not back.'

'Yeah, yeah. Well even if you're not back – yet – you haven't strayed too, far have you? I mean what's with the clinic thing? You a nurse? Don't tell me you've gone soft, that you're one of them bloody do-gooders now. Really, let's face it you're the same old Beth. Why else would you be working at the clap clinic? Just can't stay away from the trade, it obvious.'

It wasn't as if Beth didn't question herself about this very point, but there was no way she was going to discuss her choices with Carl Jacobs. Beth knew how it must look, how conflicted it must appear to be seemingly saying one thing and doing another.

But what was the point of trying to explain it to someone like Carl. He would never be willing or able to understand it.

'Carl, I am not back. I'm just here for Leah and that's all. I've moved on, I've got a good job, a new life. You can't control me anymore.'

Carl's expression showed she had found a target somewhere with him. He looked so annoyed that she slightly regretted speaking up.

Had she gone too far? It was so difficult talking to him again, even after all the years. She didn't want the situation to escalate out of control and her big mouth was possibly going to get her and Leah in to trouble here.

'Me, controlling? Fucking hell girl, I only ever looked out for you, protected you from the violent punters, from the pigs, gave you a purpose, a job.'

Yeah, by being violent and controlling, thought Beth. She didn't say anything and reached to sip the tea Leah had handed her.

An ever-increasing bundle of nerves, Leah was now shaking and dancing from one foot to another. She had spilt splashes of tea down one leg of jeans in her agitation, leaving a dark trail down her leg against the pale denim.

'Fucking sit down,' Carl growled at her, pushing her hard so that she fell back on to the sofa.

'You're doin' my head in hovering like that.'

'Sorry Carl'.

'And shut the fuck up too, I'm here to talk to Beth not you.'

'Sorry Carl.'

'Jesus, stop fucking telling me you're sorry. Here, make yourself useful and get me some smokes from the shop.'

He had taken out his wallet and now thrust a couple of notes towards her.

'Okay Carl, sor–'

Leah cut herself short, her head bobbing down. She pocketed the money Carl held up and hurried to the door.

'Leah!' Beth exclaimed, realising that she was about to be left alone with him.

Carl turned to face Beth, a quizzical smirk on his face.

Leah paused at the threshold.

'Yeah?'

Beth knew she needed to save face. Carl could already see she was rattled.

'Err, get us some biscuits eh, Leah?'

Carl chuckled unpleasantly to himself.

'Sure thing, won't be long,' said Leah as she headed out.

'So, alone at last,' said Carl.

He grinned, wickedly Beth thought. It was reminiscent of a picture from one of her childhood story books. The big bad wolf was ravenously eyeing up little Red Riding Hood, with the image of a large cooking pot on an open fire in the background.

The proximity of Carl, in this tiny room, was almost too much to bear.

'Relax Beth, seriously... it's not like I'm going to eat you.'

He leaned in close to Beth, exaggeratedly licking his tongue over his lips before baring his teeth in a ghoulish grimace.

Beth gasped and lurched backwards.

'Fucking hell, Beth, I'm only joking. Don't freak out on me.'

Beth swallowed hard trying to make her voice come out steady and strong.

'Look Carl, I'm here to see Leah, as a friend, that's all.'

'And? Did I suggest anything else? Fuck me girl, you're as suspicious as ever. Makes me think maybe that's just bullshit. Maybe you are here to poke your nose into business that don't concern you.'

'No, I –'

'Relax girl.'

Carl's mood seemed to flip back and forth. She just couldn't read him, he was still the same old Carl, that was evident, but somehow, he seemed to be even more unpleasant and confusing than she remembered. Carl started to scrabble about in his pocket.

'Here, you want a little something for those nerves?'

His words sent Beth reeling back in time. Just like the old days when he used to use that line before giving her something to take the edge off, and then sending her out to work. A sickening sense of *déjà vu* flooded over her.

'No thanks, I'm clean now.'

'Yeah, but I bet you still have that itch though. Never goes away, does it? Go on, fancy a trip down memory lane?'

Despite her abhorrence at his suggestion, she did feel something of that old familiar pull. That aching need resurfacing, just a little. This was still going to take some willpower. But she was up to it, she couldn't let herself slide back now. She shook her head. After all, this was Carl and she despised him. There was no way she was going back there, not now and most definitely not with him.

Carl shuffled his bulk along the bed, moving in closer, almost touching her. Beth felt sick, her breathing catching roughly in her throat. She could smell his aftershave and the acrid blend of cigarette smoke and last night's beer on his breathe.

'Are you sure, babe? It's a freebie, of course.'

'No, I'm good thanks.'

Carl shrugged. He remained seated next to her. Far too close for comfort. Any weakness he would pounce on. Like a cat batting seemingly half-heartedly at its prey, but prolonging its own pleasure of the moment, before the kill.

'Beth listen, I have to be honest with ya. When I saw you again down the Triangle, well it was a shock for me, and you know what I mean? It's been a while girly ain't it?'

His tone was disconcertingly soft. Beth managed to force a small smile to twitch across her mouth.

'I've missed my girl, and seeing you made me realise just how much. We were good together. You were the best, Beth. You were always special to me; you know that don't ya? I don't wanna sound like a cliché but really, to me, you were never like the other girls –'

'Carl, please stop. I don't want to talk about it. That time is the past for me. I told you, my life has changed, it's all different for me now.'

All of the illusions of reasonableness dissipated as quickly as they had arrived. The old Carl returned, true to form.

'Yeah right, like you don't miss the buzz, the excitement of it. You might think you're beyond it now but listen up, you will always – and I fucking mean always – be my girl.'

'No Carl, I was never your girl, I was just ONE of your girls, and I'm so not that person anymore, and I have a new life, a normal life where I can respect myself.'

Carl lunged, grabbing Beth by both arms.

'What are you doing? Get the fuck off me!'

'Think we're a fucking cut above. Well, think again you dumb bitch. If I want you back then you'll be back down the Triangle before you fucking know it, you get me?'

Carl dug his fingers deeper into Beth's arms, his nails sharp against her flesh, his face was up in hers, spitting the venomous words into her eyes. She could see a thick vein in his temple rising to the surface. She focused on it, remembering it. The vein would appear when he was high, was angry or had sex. Not that the intimate side of their relationship had lasted very long.

He had stopped having sex with her quite early. Unsurprisingly it had coincided with the time he had put her out on the beat. Not that she had cared much. It had always been basic with Carl. Never making love, never with any actual affection or sensitivity. When it had stopped it just felt like one less punter, one less freebie.

Still, there was that same old vein popping out in his head. A reminder of those days, of his aggression, the air of menace he could so easily conjure. This was how he had gained control of her whole life back then, the ever-present threat followed by the drugs, to seal the deal.

Fear drove a course through her and she struggled to release herself from his all too familiar grip.

'Hiya!'

Leah burst through the door.

Carl momentarily turned his head to look at her. It was long enough for Beth to pull free from his restrictive embrace. She quickly stood, straightening her now twisted clothing and made for the door.

Concealing her fluster Beth said, 'Sorry Leah, I really have to go.'

'Okay,' was all the girl could manage.

CHAPTER 13

Beth hurried down the road. The echo of the slamming door tormented her, but there was no way she could go back to the flat.

She quickly rounded the corner, desperately hoping that Carl hadn't see the direction of her escape.

When she was sure there was no longer a view from the house, she broke into a run. She raced full pelt. She didn't care where, just as long as it took her as far away from Carl as possible. She hated that she had left Leah with him. God knows what he was doing to her right now.

She had no other choice. Call it self-preservation, call it outright fear. Whatever, just as long as she was as far away from Carl as her legs would take her.

Eventually, when the adrenalin no longer overcame the aching need in her burning lungs, she slowed her pace. Beth took in her surroundings. She had stopped near the stone pillars of the entrance to a park. Perfect for her right now, a place of peace she hoped. She made her way in, forcing her pace to be sedate, calm, as she traversed the shrub lined path.

Being alone, away from the dangers that Carl presented was a relief. She found a bench and sat, breathing heavily, head in hands.

It was only then that the tears began to flow. She let them.

How long had it been since she had last cried? She was always trying to be strong, for Dad and Cassie, for everyone. It felt so good to just let go, let all the tension out and quietly bawl. The events of the last few days swirled around her and she wished she could make sense of it all.

'Beth. Hi Beth. Is everything okay?'

She flipped her head up swiftly, fearing that Carl had seen the direction she had taken and followed her. But it was Bloom and Davidson who stood on the path before her.

It was a surprise to see them, but at least she could draw breath. Knowing them, though, maybe she should have expected it. After all, they did seem to turn up wherever, whenever they liked.

However, this time she was happy it was them. Happy it wasn't Carl, at least.

Still, why the hell where they here? She felt a nudge of annoyance creeping in next to the relief. Were they tailing her or something?

'I'm fine.' A curt reply. She pretended to tame tendrils of her hair, using the opportunity to wipe the sheen of tears from her face. 'What are you doing here? How did you know I was here?'

'We didn't know it was you, Beth. Not until we got up close to you.' Abby Davidson sat down, uninvited, on the bench next to her. Beth bristled but said nothing. After all it was a public place, so she could hardly complain. 'We were in the area on another matter and we saw you. Well, we saw a lone woman sat on a park bench, clearly in some distress. We were just checking out the situation.'

'I see, okay. Well, I'm fine. There's no distress here. Everything is fine, thank you.'

'Is that the truth? Because it doesn't look like it from here. What are you doing here, alone? It's not the safest of places for a lone woman to spend the evening.'

Beth wondered if there had been another gap in time for her. She was unsure when she had left Carl and Leah at the flat, or indeed what time it was now. These gaps in her memory, she knew why they happened. She didn't want to face up to it, but she knew. All those years ago, the events back then, they had found a way of staying with her. Maybe it was because she had tried so hard to ignore it all. To move on, pretend she was over it all.

Maybe she had deluded herself a little on that score, thinking that she could just walk away and start over. Not that she was going to let the police know anything, of course.

'I'm not doing anything here. I'm out for a run and stopped to rest. That's all. Anyway, I can look after myself you know.'

'You don't look dressed for a run.'

This was annoying.

'I know. It was one of those spur of the moment things, you know what I mean.' Beth blustered to the detective.

DCI Bloom seemed to be increasingly agitated. He repeatedly checked his watch and sniffed impatiently. 'Come on Davidson, she says she fine, let's leave it at that. We have other places we need to be.'

The young DI stood up, smoothing down her jacket. 'Guv can we just have a word before we do, over there?'

Abby gestured to a spot a little further along the path.

'Alright Abby, I suppose so,' sighed Bloom, 'but this better not take long.'

They wandered off, just out of earshot of Beth. In the evening gloom she could see they were in animated conversation. Abby Davidson was gesturing enthusiastically, whilst the senior officer stood with his hands thrust into his pocket, head to one side, tapping one foot. Beth took the opportunity to pull out a tissue and a mirror. She wiped at her damp make-up smeared face, as best she could, in the fading light.

The two officers approached her once more, having concluded their discussions.

'Seems that we are heading past your place on our way. So, we can give you a lift,' said Bloom gruffly.

'No thanks, I'm fine, I can find my own way. Thanks very much.'

Beth looked off into the distance. They were being very presumptuous about which direction she might be going. Plus, she was determined not to get into another difficult conversation with the two officers.

Davidson stepped forward. 'Really Beth? Cos to us it looks like you have found yourself somewhere you don't particularly want to be. Do you even know where you are?'

Begrudgingly she had to admit to herself that she didn't know this park and she was indeed lost. Not that she was going to let on to these two though.

'Of course I know where I am! What kind of suggestion is that? I'm not some kind of idiot, or a little kid that needs looking after, you know.'

She hoped to have sounded as indignant as she felt. Under her annoyance though, she knew that their offer was definitely worth considering. After all, where the hell *was* she? In a park yes, but it was a place that was new to her, and it was getting dark.

Sometimes pride wasn't the best response to have.

'Alright Beth, calm down, we just want to help.' Davidson raised her hands in mock surrender.

'Oh, just leave her, we have places to be.' Bloom started to walk off. Exasperation passed across Davidson's face.

'Hang on, Guv. Look, Beth... last chance, no strings, just a lift, okay?'

Beth sighed as if resigned to their pressure. In truth their offer was becoming increasingly attractive in the diminishing light and growing chill of the park. 'Okay, yes okay. Thanks.'

Abby Davidson smiled and looked at Peter Bloom. The senior officer huffed, stalking off down the pathway.

'Come on then,' he called over his shoulder.

The car was still warm. Not just inside. Beth had touched the bonnet as she had moved around the vehicle to reach the back passenger door. The engine had only recently stopped ticking over.

Just happened to be passing by? Already in the park? she thought with disgust. *Yeah right, this was deliberate.*

It was clear that they must have seen her as they had driven past. Beth bet they couldn't resist turning back and coming directly to her. Still, the backseat was warmer and much more comfortable than the park bench, and she felt a whole lot safer in here. The thought of finding her way back home from the gloomy park, miles from her flat, listening to unidentified noises and seeing movements in the dimly lit foliage, was unpalatable, that was for sure.

Abby keyed the ignition and the car's dashboard flashed up its illuminated display in the darkness.

Beth settled back for the journey in the dark of the backseat.

'Hey, Beth,' Abby said throwing her voice over her shoulder as she maintained her eyes on the road ahead, 'Is everything okay, really? You did seem rather upset back there.'

Beth was exasperated. She should have known they wouldn't just give her a quiet ride home. Damn it.

'Yes, of course. Like is said, I'm fine.'

Bloom cut in. 'Really, you were a long way from home there. Isn't that near to where Carl Jacobs used to live?'

'Is it? I dunno. Guess it could be, but what of it? Just because I was passing through doesn't mean I was doing anything wrong there.'

'Did we say you were doing something wrong? Maybe you were just catching up with old friends then?'

'What's that supposed to mean?'

'Well, we know Carl still operates around that area. Maybe you felt like rekindling something –'

Beth spluttered. 'Are you mad? Me and Carl were over years ago. It wasn't exactly love's young dream, as you well know, Peter. Why would I want to do that!?'

'You've not seen Carl then, not been down there to meet him?'

'No. Let me spell it out for you. I did not go there intending to meet Carl Jacobs. I was out for a jog and stopped there for a few moments. Is that clear enough for you?'

'Okay Beth, calm down. It was just a simple question. So, you didn't intend to meet him. Does that mean you hoped to bump into him?'

'Look, what is this? What are you trying to get at here? God, it's like you lot are always deliberately trying to trip me up or something.'

'Look Beth, we aren't accusing you of anything,' said DI Davidson.

'Aren't you? You sure about that?'

'We are just investigating some matters that Carl might be involved in. You realise that you were not that far from the Triangle at that park, don't you? As you are aware, there have been some murders down there. Plus, it's not a particularly safe place to be anyway for a young woman.'

Patronising much! she thought. Their words had done nothing to appease Beth.

'Well, it bloody well sounds like you think I'm involved in something. Yeah, I knew Carl years back. It's no secret. And yeah, I was a messed-up kid back then, but seriously it was all so long ago.'

'Okay,' continued Davidson, 'it's just a little odd finding you, alone, in a park near Carl's patch. That's all we are saying.'

'Fucking hell, you don't know when to stop you lot, do you? I've told you I haven't got anything to do with Carl anymore, and I have repeatedly told you that until recently I hadn't been down to the Triangle at all in fucking years. Bloody police, you're all the same. I can assure you that I most certainly haven't got anything to do with any murders either and I would really appreciate it if you would stop harassing me.'

'Careful now Beth, you're starting to display the attitude of that girl we all used to know from down the Triangle. I thought you said you'd moved on.'

Bloom's tone was scathing.

Beth lurched forward in her seat, the seatbelt cutting into her shoulder.

'Well, if anyone would know all about the girls down there, Peter, it would be you!'

She fell back into the gloom of her seat like a petulant teenager. Davidson shot Bloom a hard glance but said nothing.

The remainder of the journey was passed without further conversation. The burble of the police radio was the only sound to interruption the stony silence. There was a mutual sense of relief when they reached Beth's block of flats. Beth climbed out of the car without a word. She made sure to slam the car door hard, behind her.

'Guv, what was that about?'

Bloom passed his hands across his face pushing the sagging skin up, only for it to drop back to its usual hangdog position. 'Leave it, Abby.'

'But...'

'I said leave it. Please. It was a long time ago and I'm way too tired to go into it now.'

'Sorry, Guv.'

'Let's just get back to the station. You still have that paperwork to do and then we need to get down to the Triangle again, see if there's any of the girls around that would be willing to talk to us.'

Abby looked across at her boss once more in silence. He sat in profile against the streetlight filtering in through the car window. A brooding brow, sitting atop the Roman nose. The thin line of his firmly closed lips She could see there would be no progress with him on the matter. Not after that little confrontation with Beth. She started the engine.

'Okay Guv, whatever you say.'

CHAPTER 14

Back at the station, Abby found that she couldn't let the altercation settle. The veiled accusations Bloom and Beth had thrown at each other, the suggestions that their words planted in her mind, gnawed at her like a bellyache.

She adopted a light tone, jovial almost as she asked some of her fellow officers just why Bloom had such a miserable attitude. It didn't get her any further forward in understanding him. Some shrugged off her questions, making excuses that allowed them to wander away. Others huffed and stumbled over a response, saying that he was just another grumpy old man.

But Abby wasn't wearing that. It couldn't be as simple as that. It had to be more than just one more middle-aged copper, close to retirement age, having a gripe, feeling jaded about the job. After all, there were bloody loads of them here doing that.

No. This felt different.

Her intuition had kicked in a few times lately. She kept that to herself. She'd made the mistake of expressing how intuition had helped her before and got laughed out of the custody suite. Cold hard facts, she'd been told, none of that touchy-feely nonsense.

But right now, that sense in her was tingling away like crazy, telling her to dig deeper.

She decided to tackle Peter again. Not that she ever called him by his first name to his face. It had been a surprise when Beth Hooper had called him Peter during the car journey. She hadn't realised they knew each other well enough for such intimacy. Abby was always deferential. He was her boss, her Guv or just plain old Bloom.

She found him at his desk. He was tapping doggedly with two fingers at his keyboard. Back in the day, when he had joined the force, they had a typing pool for tasks like this. Times may have changed, the typists long gone, but he hadn't. He remained determinedly old school and had never bothered, or rather vigorously resisted the need to learn how to Touch Type.

Abby eyed him, weighing up whether or not this was a good time to broach the matter. Bloom was prickly at the best of times. He needed to be approached as you would when trying tame an irritable feral animal. She would edge her way towards him, gain his trust and tease the truth out of him.

He seemed oblivious to her presence so she loudly cleared her throat.

'It's a complex situation for those girls down the Triangle, eh Guv?'

Bloom just grunted and continued to stare fixedly at his computer screen. Abby wasn't going to let that put her off. She persisted.

'I mean, it's such a tough existence for them, I just can't believe that any of the women doing sex work down there actually choose it, or that they ever expected to have ended up down there.'

Bloom looked up at her for a moment. He opened his mouth as if to speak but instead pushed the tip of his pen between his lips and clamped his teeth down on it. He returned his gaze to the report he was typing up.

'I just wish we could do more to support them,' Abby continued unabashed.

Bloom didn't look up at her this time but he pulled the pen from between his lip and finally spoke. 'This job is not an opportunity to live out your personal moral crusades, Davidson.'

Abby was pleased that he was at least responding, even if it was to reprimand her. 'I know Guv, it's just that I feel for them.'

'Go and be a bloody social worker then,' snapped Bloom.

'Guv, I don't mean it like that, it's just that their situation, well... it's about basic human dignity isn't it.'

Bloom sighed, throwing his pen down hard. It ricocheted around the desk chiming a musical tone against his half empty coffee mug. 'I get that Abby, I do, more than most in here.' He gestured with a sharp tip of his head. 'But take it from me, experience has taught me that you can't help em. They don't want it and it's not our place to give it.'

'I'm sorry Guv, and I don't mean to argue with you, but I don't see why not. Surely, we have a responsibility to try to help, or at least point them in the direction of other agencies that can?'

'No, I don't see it like that and neither should you. You are a police officer and one that should be well aware of the implications of that role and the need to follow police protocol and procedure at all times. We have our own jobs to do and we aren't here to clear up the messes people make of their lives.'

'But Gu –'

'Abby! Enough. There's reports need writing and call-backs to make. This discussion is over. Get back to work.'

Abby knew him well enough to know when to shut up. He'd closed himself up now, she could see it in his body language. He was hunched back over his desk, almost hugging it. His face set in a stern mask was once more focused on the screen.

She wasn't giving up though, just letting it go for today.

It was now very clear to her that there was something embedded deep that was an influence on his general demeanour. The tone of his voice, the way he had been so defensive on the subject, told her that her intuition had been right. Bloom had alluded to his experience of the Triangle, so there just had to be more to this whole matter.

Abby may not have been on the force as long as Bloom, but she had people skills that he didn't and those had successfully helped her to pull details out of interviewees before now. She just needed time to deploy them on her boss.

Later, she thought. *This will keep.*

She returned to her own computer. Disheartened to see a fresh mountainous list of emails in her inbox.

'Abby.' Bloom called over to her.

She quickly rose from her desk and walked back down the office.

'There's been another one.'

'Another?'

'Yes, a third body. A male, has been found down at the Triangle. Same M.O. it seems. Elderly man found in his car with an arm injury. Come on, we have work to do.'

'Yes Guv, ready when you are.'

CHAPTER 15

Beth had the morning off. After paying an early visit to the hospital ward to see her father, she was unsure of how to spend the free time. A wander through the city centre streets seemed the only option. Vaguely staring into shop windows, doubtful that there was anything she really wanted to look at, let alone buy.

Eventually, she meandered her way closer to a favourite cafe. The place had always appealed to her with its colourful frontage and large windows. A perfect spot to watch the world go by.

The wood panelled door led on to an eclectically furnished interior. A rush of warm food and coffee smells greeted her, accompanied by a cheery hello from the cafe owner, which sealed the deal. Positioning herself at a vacant table, Beth bent to place her bag at her feet. A very close clearing of a throat made her look up with a start.

Josh Simpson was standing next to the table.

'Hello again, I didn't realise you frequented this place.'

Beth quickly pushed back the hair that had fallen across her face. A strand had clumsily caught between her lips. 'Er yeah, hi. Yeah, I come here quite a lot. Not seen you in here before though.'

Josh laughed a little. 'We must come at different times then, cos I'm quite the regular too.'

'Yeah, guess we must.'

'Mind if I join you?'

For a moment she was unsure. She usually liked to sit and drift in thought. But what was the harm? It was a public place. He could sit anywhere he chose to. Beth nodded casually. 'Yeah, sure.'

Josh placed his cup and plate on the table. He pushed off his coat, to leave it hanging awkwardly over the back of his chair. He sat down heavily, jarring the table and spilling his coffee a little. A flurry of muttered curses accompanied his frantic mopping up. Beth sat back, watching him. Eventually, he caught her eye.

'Sorry.'

She shrugged. 'Better your drink than mine.'

They grinned amiably at each other. The cafe owner brought Beth's usual coffee and pastry over to the table. Beth moved them deliberately out of Josh's reach with a wry smile. She was happy to note that he took this humorously. They exchanged a few pleasantries about their surrounding and the weather, laughing at the Britishness of their conversation. It felt relaxed. However, Josh soon steered matters to the theme of their last conversation.

After sipping his coffee a few times, he said, 'I found our conversation really interesting the other day.'

'Yeah?'

'Yes, I would like to say thank you again. I know a lot of people don't trust the press, think we are as bad as politicians, or worse. So, I appreciate that you gave me a chance to explain myself.'

She knew there was an element of flattery in what he was saying but she resisted the urge to pick up on it, instead simply responding, 'No problem.'

Josh continued. 'I know you can't give me details about individuals –'

Beth cocked her head to one side, looking pointedly at him.

'No, it's okay, I totally get it. It's just that, I wondered about you giving me a more general view, as someone involved, I mean. Picking up from where we left off really.'

She shuffled awkwardly in her seat. She wanted to say yes, but at the same time she had concerns. She had enough going on without putting herself out there publicly. 'Hmm, I don't know about that. I'm not sure I could do that. I have to remain impartial and consider confidentiality. It is so important in my job. I couldn't go "on the record" as they say. It just wouldn't feel right.'

98

'No, I was thinking more like you giving me a wider view on the sex industry, for my research. I absolutely would not be quoting you directly. It would just be background for my own understanding.'

It sounded plausible and she did have thoughts she would like to share. If he was guaranteeing that this was not some kind of interview and that she would not to be named as his source, then maybe it wasn't so bad?

'Okay, maybe I can work with that. I don't think I get your angle though. What is it you are trying to focus on? I mean, the world of sex work is huge, so varied. You could end up writing a thesis on it, never mind a single article. So, what is it you are looking at? Prostitution, the beat, brothels, the internet, telephone sex, lap dancing clubs, sex shows, porn films, escort agencies, fetish, male, female? See what I mean, it's a vast topic area to start delving into, and that's not the half of it.'

'Well, for us, back at the news agency, it started out with complaints from local residents. About the red-light area and the impact it was having on their lives. That's what my editor tasked me with. But then the more I looked into it the more I wanted to write a balanced piece. Maybe even a series of pieces about it. Sure, the impact on residents' lives is significant and really important. It totally needs to be acknowledged, but I want to understand how it is for the sex workers as well. Why they do it, and who they do it for, you know? I'm not looking to create some gutter press shock story. I want it to be balanced, and real.'

Beth stirred her coffee thoroughly as she mulled over where to begin. Eventually she put the spoon back down on her plate.

'Okay, well first off, I do not subscribe to the usual media portrayal of prostitution. Working in the sex industry is much more complex than that. I think that whilst it isn't always as melodramatic as is suggested in the news and on TV, it is true to say that there are a great many sex workers who haven't chosen it as their life path, but are doing so for a variety of reasons. But, in fairness there are also some, a much smaller number in my view, that have elected to do sex work. This is kind of what I mean when I say its complex. There's no 'one size fits all' to sex work, no pun intended, and no easy stereotype role to fit into. The same goes for why people stay in that type of work. Yes, occasionally its choice, but there's also a lot of coercion and drugs keeping people in that cycle.'

She was warming to her subject now.

'The thing is, there will always be people who want to pay for sex, and those that will sell it. What I would like to see is a more mature attitude to the matter, an acceptance that it is a reality and not something to deny exists or try to hide away in the darkest parts of our towns and cities. I'm not advocating it being brought into communities or seeing sex workers on our high streets, but it needs to be decriminalised, made safer for those doing the job.'

'In what sort of ways?' Josh interjected.

'Well, for me the main concerns are about safety. For the women working the beat. The fact is that they are often controlled, be it by other people, debt, drugs or a combination of all three. There's also the danger of attacks by punters or those that treat the beat like some kind of weird tourist destination. The sorts of things I am thinking of are organised unions and safe brothels, run by sex workers themselves rather than being controlled by others profiting from it. The fact that we have a tolerant view from the authorities in our city is a positive acknowledgment of the fact that sex work is a reality, but that in itself is not enough. And let's face it: it causes other sorts of problems.'

'Yes, like the impact on the residents living close to the area.'

'Yes, definitely. It must be really tough living with those activities on your doorstep. But it's also that the women are pretty much left to their own devices by the police. The tolerance by the authorities has reduced their presence in the area. It's a double-edged sword of sorts. This decriminalisation, whilst making arrests less likely also makes sex workers more vulnerable to random attacks and abuse.'

Beth paused, feeling that she may have ranted a little. It was just so close to home; she couldn't help but feel passionate about it.

'Sorry, I kind of got on my soapbox there.'

Josh shock his head. 'No, absolutely not. What you said made a lot of sense. Very thought provoking.'

The pair lapsed into silence. Beth returned her attention, pulling apart the flakes of pastry still on her plate, wondering if she had said too much. It seemed as if Josh wanted to say more. He repeatedly raised his head and opened his mouth, before letting his chin drop again.

Finally, she couldn't bear the tension any longer. 'What is it Josh? You obviously have something else you want to say.'

'Sorry, Beth.'

He was visibly trembling now, his fingers knocking against the tabletop.

'It's just... well, I don't know how to quite begin this.'

Beth sighed, impatiently. It seemed to prompt him, in the wrong way.

'No look it's nothing, really... it's fine, don't worry about it.'

'Clearly that's not the case. You can't leave me hanging like that wondering what you were going to say. So, just say it.'

Josh shuffled in his seat. Straightening his spine, he returned her gaze. 'Okay, here's how it is. When we first met, down the Triangle I mean, you remember when I came over and talked to you?'

She nodded.

'Well, you also remember that I told you about my friend at college, yeah?'

Shit, she knew where this was going. 'Yeah, I remember.'

'Well, I kind of got the impression, Jesus how do I say this –'

'Just say it Josh, say it.'

'Okay, sorry. Well, look can I ask you? Were you... did you work down there at some point? On the street, I mean. Did you work the beat?'

He slumped back down in his seat, as if embarrassed by his own questioning.

Beth had felt that this might be coming. It was to be expected. After all he was a journalist, well used to considering all of the possible trails a story could go down. She just hadn't expected to be raised quite so quickly though.

But here it was. In some ways Josh raising it now made it easier for her. There was clearly some form of friendship developing between them. So, it was undoubtedly a good thing that it had happened now, before they had gotten any closer. It would be a whole lot easier for him to walk away and a whole lot easier for her to watch him do so at this stage.

Best to head this off then.

'I did. It was years ago though, when I was a teenager. But yes, I worked the beat. I'm not ashamed of it, you know.'

'Right. I see.'

'You have no right to judge me, Josh.'

'No, God, no I'm not. Believe me.'

'I was young, stupid, flattered by the attentions of someone. Manipulated by them. But it was a lifetime ago.'

'No Beth, I understand and I didn't mean to offend you in any way. Or to judge you. Quite the opposite, I can assure you. I just wanted to be sure, didn't want to presume and I also want to be clear in saying that it does not change my view of you at all.'

She studied him closely as he spoke, looking for clues. Was he being truthful? She really hoped she could believe in what he was saying. There was always that tiny nagging doubt in her, that pin-prick of negativity. Born of self-preservation. He looked so genuine, earnest. But good looks and kind words could be deceivers. They could lead you astray. Life was so different now though. She needed to remember that not everyone wanted something from her.

She managed a small smile and Josh smiled back. Relief cutting through his features. Still, she felt it was time to cut this conversation short.

'Thanks, I appreciate that, but I really need to go now.'

'Ah shame, oh well, maybe we can get together some other time, have another coffee or go for a drink?'

She felt flushed and hoped it didn't show in her skin. 'Yes, that would be lovely, thank you. Bye for now then.'

'Bye, Beth.'

She rose to leave, feeling his eyes on her as she made for the door. Finally, outside she realised she had been holding her breath. She was acting like a teenager with a crush. She chided herself about it, but it did feel oddly good all the same.

CHAPTER 16

The Scene of Crime Unit was already busy, filling the small dead-end street. A host of officers, vehicles and equipment greeted Davidson and Bloom on their arrival.

A light rain had started to dampen the air. The pair felt somewhat reluctant to leave the warm cocoon of their car. The very end of the street had been cordoned off with tape and the two detectives quickly flashed their ID at the young unformed officer manning the temporary barrier. He deferentially inclined his head and raised the cordon. Bloom and Davidson passed under and entered the street.

A large tent had been erected over the found vehicle. It wasn't until Bloom and Davidson were up close that they were able to see that both the driver and passenger doors of the vehicle were wide open. Officers in white overalls bustled around, dipping in and out of the open car.

'Do we have any witness? Who called in it?' asked Davidson.

Bloom looked around at the buildings that spanned the sides the narrow road. 'A security guard, I believe. Bloke called Harry Wood. He's well known to us. Has worked around here for decades. Lots of empty premises here, from the looks of it.' He waved a hand this way and that indicating the boarded-up doorways and gaping black mouths of burnt-out windows around them.

'Yes. Nice quiet spot to do business. Not much in the way of natural surveillance here, Guv.'

'None at all, I'm reckoning,' Bloom grunted.

By now they had walked the full length of the street. They returned a short distance to stand, across from each other, on either side of the car. It was parked at the end of road facing a footpath and a small patch of scrubby grass. At the very end of the street was a towering brick wall, and other than the Scene of Crime van it was the only vehicle parked down the cut off little street. Both detectives bent in under the open sides of the tent to peer in through the open car doors.

'Looks like this one struggled, Guv,' Davidson noted.

Bloom nodded his response, his eyes busy roaming the body, as if trying to take in every detail. Before them, the occupier of the car lay awkwardly, leaning to one side. It was clear that he had been in the driver's seat, but he appeared to have either fallen over onto the passenger seat or had possibly been reaching in that direction.

An elderly man, grey of hair, with sagging jowls and spectacles. These had been knocked to an almost jocular angle on his face, giving the scene a macabre sense of comedy. His clothing was dishevelled, with his trousers unzipped and underwear unbuttoned. His genitals lay exposed, like a small pile of greying meat in his lap. A dark stain had spread across both trouser legs of his faun-coloured slack. Abby Davidson presumed that his bladder must have emptied at the point of death, if not before.

Interestingly, the man's left arm was stretched out full length, as if he had been attempting to clasp at the passenger door or possibly the last person to have occupied the other front seat. Davidson could see a bead of blood had formed, like a jewel set against a crease of loose flesh on his inner arm. She moved in closer, inspecting the blood. A puncture wound was discernible in the slack skin, beneath the rust-coloured stain.

'I think it could be another needle job, Guv.' Davidson pointed to the site of what she thought to be the wound.

'Hmm. Other than speculation and that he does look like he was here to meet a prostitute, there's nothing yet that says that this is a murder scene. He could have come here and willingly taken drugs, for it then to have just gone wrong. Horribly for him.

But still, it does look like a potential overdose. His companion, if there was one, might have been fearful of getting caught up in it, if they had met here for paid sex. They might have just run off because of that, rather than anything else. Callous, of course, leaving a dying man like that, but it's a possibility.'

Bloom stood and turned to talk to an approaching Scene of Crime Officers.

'Abby, come over here a moment and have a look at what the SOCOs found.' He was holding up a plastic evidence bag the other officer had handed to him. Inside, Abby Davidson could clearly see the outline of a hypodermic needle.

'That's a stroke of luck then. Can your team get anything from it, do you reckon?'

'Hopefully,' replied the over-all clad Scene of Crime Officer. 'If we are fortunate enough we might get some cellular material and I think some chemical traces too, maybe even blood from the look of the syringe chamber. We need to analysis it back at base. We already have some fingerprints from it, and from the steering wheel and passenger door as well.'

'Can you estimate a time of death yet?'

'Well, estimate would be the right word for it as the engine may have been left running for some time. His body temperature could have been kept higher than you would expect by the warmth of the car. But, push comes to shove, I would say, five maybe six hours ago for time of death. We will know more when his body is examined in detail.'

'And do we have a name for the victim?' Davidson pushed.

The Scene of Crime Officer pulled out another evidence bag.

'The details in his wallet say it's a Nigel Franks. Here, we have his driver's licence picture. Confirms that this appears to be the same man.'

Bloom was quick to interject. 'Subject to an official identification.'

'Of course,' replied the Scene of Crime Officer.

'Looks like it could be either foul play or misadventure to me,' Bloom continued.

Davidson felt sure it must be the former. 'But Guv, surely as this is so much like those other cases, this death has to be linked to them? There are too many similarities that we can't ignore. This has to be considered to be foul play here, in my view, Sir.'

'Probably so Davidson, but as you are aware, we do need to wait for the evidence to be processed. No good jumping the gun here and panicking people unnecessarily now, is there.'

Davidson felt annoyed at her own impatience and at Bloom. She really needed to learn to curb it, but she felt sure that this was a linked case. She tried not to sound disappointed.

'No, Guv.'

Bloom could see her keenness; knew she was a good officer. She simply needed to reign herself in sometimes. Given enough time she would learn. He looked kindly at her.

'Listen Abby, your responses are good but you're sometimes a bit too thirsty for the result. Half the battle is getting the evidence, putting it in order and making sure it's robust, that it is gonna stick. You're also most probably correct as well, of course.'

Davidson grinned. 'Thanks Guv, and duly noted.'

'Okay, well, let's get on with the job, then shall we?'

CHAPTER 17

'Coming for a drink, Beth?' said Jenny. 'Everyone else is going. We'd all love you to join us all.'

Beth was tidying the clinic room after another full day of appointments and walk-ins. She paused, her arms full of leaflets and looked up to see the friendly face of her boss. Jenny was leaning her head and shoulder around the open door. It had been a tough few days and Beth was dog tired.

Jenny must surely have noted the look on her face but clearly wasn't ready to give up. She moved forward to perch on the edge of the consultation bed.

Beth had thus far found the senior nurse to be very approachable. Jenny was a young manager and appeared to like tackling issues head on. Beth appreciated the frankness of her approach.

Jenny was watching as Beth moved around the room, straightening leaflets and loosely folded a couple of blankets, ready for the laundry.

'You know Beth that we all consider you to be a valued member of the team here.'

Beth felt a flush of embarrassment. She was not used to compliments, welcome as this was. 'Thanks, and I do love working here.'

'Good, I'm pleased to hear it. I think you have brought a lot to the role here and I have a feeling you have more to give. You have a great attitude Beth and to be frank you've given us all some food for thought.'

Beth was cautiously curious. 'Have I? In what way?'

'Well, you and I have of course talked about your background and you have made no secret of it to us all. I and the department have very much welcomed the openness you demonstrated. In some ways, although please don't think we want to use you like some kind of poster girl, but in some respects, you have had a positive impact on breaking down stereotypes and prejudice within the department.'

'I thought everyone who worked here was pretty open minded though. I kind of expected that to be the norm here, you know, with the type of jobs we all do.'

Jenny nodded.

'Well yes, I agree that the team generally is, but there's always instances where we could do with a sensitivity check, right?'

Jenny had fought Beth's corner hard when she had applied to work at the clinic. Back then there had been those that would have frowned on her past employment and drug history. Not Jenny though. She had seen through it all and had positively encouraged Beth in the interview.

'I agree, none of us is perfect, or always knows the right thing to do.'

'Yes true, but I think with you there is an element of advocacy that some of us here just don't have. I don't mean this to sound in any way bad, but, well you've been there, done that, if you know what I mean. Sorry Beth, that doesn't sound as good as it did in my head. But you do understand what I'm saying right?'

Beth did. After all, it was the very reason she had wanted to do this job in the first place. 'It's okay, I totally get it, and I appreciate being part of the team here.'

Jenny saw her chance. 'So, that being the case, how about that drink down the pub then? Come on… join me and the others. Just one, eh, that's all I'm asking? Show your face. They are a pretty friendly lot and you might actually find it better than you anticipate you know, maybe even enjoyable.'

Beth could see Jenny's wasn't going to give up easily. What the hell, it wouldn't hurt.

'Okay, but it been a tough week and I'm longing for my bed so just one, yeah.'

Jenny nodded; her face beamed in victory. 'Great! Let's go then.'

The pub was more like a modern bar than a traditional hostelry. Not really Beth's kind of place, but she was here now so best to try to make the best of the situation. The place was packed out. The air seemed dense. A heady cocktail of perfumes and aftershave, covering the underlying sent of stale beer and the toilets. It was stuffy and oppressive.

Beth surveyed the room. There were people pushing and shoving at the bar, bellowing into each other's ears above the loud dance track pumping out, dancing and flirting with each other. Just what 'normal' people would do on a Friday night, she supposed. But Beth just felt deeply awkward and wished she hadn't agreed to come. She didn't feel like one of them. Alone in a crowd, she was not in the mood for inane chatter. Too late though, a cold glass of gin and tonic on ice was thrust into her hand.

Resigned to making the best of it she plastered on a smile and mouthed her thanks to Jenny. Maybe the gin would perk her up, she thought, and for a short while she did manage to engage with her colleagues. Joining in with their loud banter about work and their home lives. But the incessant pressure of people in the bar, the jostling and ever-increasing noise level was proving too much for her tired head.

'Excuse me a moment,' Beth said to her workmates.

She put down her drink and made her way to the beer garden at the rear of the pub. Thankfully there was only a small handful of people out here, a few lone smokers and a small group of young men deep in conversation apparently about a football match. They all looked at her briefly as she stepped out to join the, before returning either to their conversation or to the contemplation of their pints. She was thankful to be left to her own devices for a while. The low hum of the smoker's conversations was a backdrop, but least it wasn't as loud and oppressive as the voices, or the competing thump of the music, that she had been putting up with inside the bar.

Despite the hazy fog of cigarette smoke in the still air of enclosed beer garden, Beth breathed deeply. She managed to regain a little composure. Still, in her current mood, she knew that this place wasn't for her. Best to drink up and go. She headed back inside to find her drink and Jenny.

'I'm going to go after this one, Jen. I'm just not feeling it this evening.'

Jenny groaned, a look of resigned disappointment on her face. 'Okay love, I understand, thanks for at least making the effort to come out anyway. Plus, there will be other nights out so don't go thinking you've got away with it.'

Beth laughed, slugged back her now warm drink and briefly hugged Jenny. The crowded bar remained too loud with chatter to allow people to hear her, so she mouthed and waved her goodbyes to the rest of her team.

Out on the street, Beth felt she could breathe again. She made her way to the nearest bus stop. She was thankful that the circular bus passed by both the pub and her block of flats. She had done her best in the bar, but she was extremely happy to be about to make her journey home.

The bus came quickly and after allowing a number of noisy, evident partygoers to disembark, she was relieved to board it and find a double seat to herself. The chill of the evening had caused a mist of condensation on the interior of the bus windows. It was something she hated about public transport. Even as a nurse she had her limits and the blend of multiple people's breath and sweat was usually an unpalatable human cocktail to her. But today, she was too tired to be uptight about it. Since leaving the pub her energy levels had dropped even further. She now felt overly warm and out of sorts. Just not really herself. Home and bed were most definitely calling to her.

Beth pressed her hands to the cool damp glass. When this proved not to be sufficient, she pressed her forehead to it, feeling its chill penetrate and spread across the skin on her face. The condensation had increased as more people had boarded the bus. Now the misting was running in small rivulets down the glass and her face. Unusually, she didn't care. It felt good against her skin and she closed her eyes. Just for a moment, she told herself.

The sharp breaking of the bus jolted Beth awake. She looked out of the clearer windows at the front.

Shit! With a sense of panic, she realised she had missed her stop. Only by one but still, shit!

'Wait, please, hold up, I need to get off please,' she called to the driver as he started to close the doors.

Beth pulled herself heavily from the seat. She felt drunk. But how could she be after just one drink? Sure, she hadn't eaten since lunch time, but it had only been one gin in the bar. Even if it had hit her system straightaway it would have just made her a bit woozy. Not like. This felt like she had been on a full on 24-hour bender.

'Thank you.'

She was shocked to hear herself slurring her words to the driver. Embarrassed, she scurried forward, to step clumsily down from the bus and onto the darkened street. Staggering a little, Beth set off back down the road towards her block of flats.

Damn, what the hell is wrong with me? she thought.

The street was empty with the exception of one other person. They were walking some distance back from her. They seemed to be heading in the same direction, but Beth's main concern remained getting home as soon as she could. She felt so strange. Like this was not real, or she was watching herself in a dream. Oddly disconnected, she didn't feel all that concerned that there was an unknown person out on the darkened street with her.

Anyway, this was a residential area, and there were plenty of lights on in the windows that she passed. Being a woman, out after dark, on a street with a stranger, wasn't a good thing, even for someone of her experience. But when you didn't feel totally in control of yourself the potential danger was doubled. Despite her lax attitude to the situation her intuition had somehow kicked in. It pushed her to quicken her pace, despite her feelings of disconnection and fatigue.

The walker behind her, speeded up to match her stride. Shit. Was she imagining it or were they actually following her? Even trying to catch up with her? She felt so spaced out she just couldn't tell and she didn't dare turn around, let alone stop to challenge them. She just wanted to be in the safety of her block, behind lock and key.

Beth was finding walking an increasing struggle. Her legs were achingly heavy and it felt like wading through deep water. Whatever was causing this was really taking control of her now, both physically and mentally. Her ability to focus on the street ahead was diminishing with each step. The normally cosy illumination of the house windows she passed now blurred into neon strips of light. Her body didn't belong to her anymore and she stumbled over her own feet, forcing her jelly-like muscles to keep her upright.

Should she stop, stagger up one of the footpaths and bang on someone's door for help?

No, keep going, she was nearly there now.

One last push.

She reached her doorway and fumbled for her keys in her bag. The footsteps in the street echoed around her. Maybe it was her panic or the debilitated state of consciousness, heightening the situation but it seemed as if the figure following her had begun to run. She wasn't sure if any of it was real. All she was sure of was that she needed to act, fast.

Desperately she struggled with her bundle of keys, her anxiety turning her fingers into useless rubbery appendages.

Finally, the right one! But where was the lock hole, damn it. Beth fumbled, running her fingers and the key head over the door frame.

'Fuck it, come on, come on –' she muttered to herself.

Finally, the key slid into the lock. She turned it and gripping hard on the door handle, lurched forward into the lobby. The door slammed loudly behind her.

Beth turned her head to look back at through the glazed panel in the door.

She saw a figure.

Even with blurred vision she could see what appeared to be a male form. Standing across the street under the trees. The street lighting was set against a tall stone wall under the heavy tree cover. It created long dancing shadows broken by triangles of soft light. The figure was standing forward of the street lighting, dark, hooded. She could not make out the face.

Fear gagged her. It filled her mouth, taking her breath. All she could emit was a desperate gasp.

Who was that and why hide their face? Could it be Carl?

Beth watched horrified as the figure stepped forward. They paused, as if staring back at her. Then suddenly, the man set off running back down the street.

Relief rushed over her. Despite this, whatever was in her system kept her breath heavy and laboured. Beth was really struggling to keep herself conscious, but at least she had made it inside. She would normally have expected her body's adrenalin to have straightened her out. It certainly had in the past when she had been drunk or wasted and had found herself in dodgy situations. But this wasn't like just being drunk. This, whatever it was, had a stronger hold on her and she was losing the fight with it. It was wearing her down.

It seemed to take her an age to climb the stairs to her floor. Finally, Beth made it to her front door. Again, she found herself doing battle with her keys. before finally being able to enter the flat.

The sound of bells ringing greeted her. Bright peals, echoing and fading in and out, over and over again. That's lovely, she thought, and managed to push the door shut behind her. She heard the latch drop. Beth staggered again and leant against the hallway wall. Stretching out one arm, she reached towards the musical chimes. Dizzy and straining, she desperately wanted to embrace the beautiful tones. It was annoying how the music kept gliding out of reach. Fading far away into a darkness that enveloped everything.

CHAPTER 18

Beth awoke. She was lying awkwardly on the hall floor. It took a few moments to get her bearings. Her head, clouded from an unsettling dream. Images of overflowing water and broken glass still pushed through. Her neck and back were stiff and one arm felt oddly numb. She had to shake it hard to draw some life back in to the slack limb.

Last night? It was a still a jumbled mess.

She remembered being in the bar, then flashes of the bus journey. The misted windows and slow chug of the engine. The dark street. Then, the figure.

Someone, out on the street with her. Someone following her. After that, there was nothing until she had awoken groggy and crumpled on her hall carpet. Anxiety dragged in her belly. It was yet another occasion where there were blank points in her memory.

Pushing herself to stand, and stretch aching limbs, Beth lumbered her way to the living room. The answer phone was flashing its blue light at her. Four messages. Who had a landline these days? She only kept it because of Dad. He steadfastly refused to engage with modern technology. Even when she had offered to buy him a mobile phone, and pay for his line rental, he had still declined. This meant filtering out all those irritating cold callers and now that Dad was so very ill, it made her nervous every time the phone rang.

She had her finger poised over the retrieve button when the phone sprung into life, pealing demandingly. Beth grabbed the handset and pressed it to her ear.

'Hello?' she croaked.

'Beth, at fucking last! I've been trying to get hold of you all night! Don't you ever answer your phone? I tried your mobile and your landline. Where the hell have you been?'

Her sister, Cassie, who sounded furious.

'Ow Cassie, tone it down, my head –'

'Don't tell me to fucking tone it down, I'm bloody sick of your attitude. You are never damn well available when I need to speak to you. It's like you think it's alright to just leave everything to me, to swan off lord knows where, doing who knows what. Really Beth, grow up. You can't simply go through life just doing whatever the hell you like.'

'Hey Cassie, I'm sorry but –' Beth tried to interrupt, but her sister talked over her, ignoring any attempt and an explanation.

'Don't bother with your pathetic apologies and don't bother to come up with some elaborate excuse. I can tell that you are hung-over from the sound of your voice. Just get yourself down to the hospital now. Dad's had a fall. It's not good.'

Beth's stomach flipped, pushing a wave of alcohol flavoured nausea up her throat. 'Oh no. Is he okay?'

But Cassie had put the phone down on her. No further explanations and no goodbyes. A moment of panic set in. Cassie hadn't told her enough about the fall, so naturally she presumed the worst. Was Dad.... She could barely allow herself to think it, but was he, dead? Her sister had deliberately withheld information. All the better to panic Beth. She could imagine Cassie at the other end of the phone, a weird look of triumph on her face as she fed Beth just enough information to get her rattled. Even at a time like this she couldn't help sticking the knife in. But still, Dad. Christ, what was she going to find when she arrived at the hospital?

She was hardly in a fit state to see him either. Last night's events were playing over in her head, as she struggled to make sense of them. If only she could fill in those blank parts of the evening. She was long since used to times when her brain would zone out. Not that she had done anything to find out why. That was too big and scary a prospect. Anyway, this had felt different to her usual memory lapses. She could only conclude that either she was ill, or her drink had been spiked. Now she had come around a bit, physically she didn't feel too bad. Just a dull ache in her back and a fuzzy head. Mentally was another matter. It was very unsettling.

She thought back to the pub. Everyone says you shouldn't leave your drink unattended, and yes, she had foolishly left her glass on the table to go and get some air. But she thought she had left it with friends, her work mates. Could it have happened then? Someone *must* have put something in her drink. It was the only logical explanation. But who? Surely not one of her colleagues?

No, she didn't want to think that was possible. Anyway, the pub had been packed with people. It could have been anyone. The last thing she needed right now was to lose faith in the people close to her.

Still, that could mean an unknown person. Someone in the pub, who had been watching her. An opportunist taking their chance to lace her glass. To do her harm. Beth shuddered at the thought of how things could have turned out.

Was the person on her street last night the drink spiker? Was it worse if it wasn't and there were two people out to get her in some way last night?

Worry crouched heavily in her gut. She desperately wanted to fold herself up and crawl into a corner.

Christ, she needed to stop thinking like this. Her mind was racing with possibilities, all bad!

'Come on, get it together,' she told herself.

Cassie's words had, as ever, stung her. As they were intended to. Their relationship had always been a complex one and she was well used to barbed exchanges with her sister. Cassie clearly felt that Beth was not shouldering her share of the responsibility with regard to their father and his worsening condition. She did try.

But Cas always wanted to play the martyr, so she would never win. Not her sister's fault, Beth supposed. Cassie had played the role of mother from an early age. The sisters had only ever really had the care of their father. That can't have been easy.

Their mother had died when Beth had been very small. A heart attack, she had been told. She had never known the woman who had given birth to her. She was just a pretty young woman dressed in old fashioned clothes in grainy photos. Beth had done her best to build up a character for her from the old photos and family stories. But she could never be sure if it lived up to the real person, of if that even mattered.

Cassie was ten years her senior. Stepping up to parent Beth at such a young age meant her sister had missed out on a lot of the normal teenage years. No wonder she was resentful. On top of that Beth had gone well and truly wild as a teenager. All the while Cassie had remained steady, reliable. Sensible old Cassie.

Still, it was galling to hear Cassie having a go at her yet again. Particularly when she felt that she did as much as she could for their father. It wasn't easy working full time and caring for someone so sick. When Dad had been taken into the ward it had all felt a bit more manageable. Plus, Dad being at the hospital meant Beth had been able to see more of him.

Needing to shrug off the thoughts of the old family rivalry and get herself together, she showered. The flow of warm water soothed the growing headache and softened the tension in her back muscles. Sleeping on the floor was not conducive to a good night's rest, especially when potentially drugged by an unknown substance.

CHAPTER 19

Beth was lucky to catch a bus straight away. Taking her seat, the vibration of her phone against her hip signalled the arrival of a new message.

- *Where the hell r u?*

Cassie.

Before she had time to text back the phone buzzed again.

- *Sick of u leaving everything to me.*

Christ, give me a chance, Beth thought angrily. She tapped hard on the phone screen.

- *On my way.*

Again, the phone pulsed in her hand.

- *Same old story from u. Hurry up.*

She took a couple of moments to scroll back through the texts Cassie had sent her the night before. After the initial one, advising of their father's fall, they were all in a similar vein to the latest ones Cassie had sent. Same old accusatory tone she had come to expect from her sister.

The bus was nearly at the hospital grounds. It wasn't worth texting back now. She wouldn't get a pleasant reply from Cassie anyway, not when she was so evidently annoyed with her. Cassie just had a lifelong downer on her.

Beth pressed the bell to signal to the bus to stop.

*

Cassie looked up as Beth entered the small side ward. A flash of irritation passed over her face, before her features settled back into a non-committal mask. Their father lay in one of two beds in the small room. The room had low lighting and was painted in calm colours. The other bed was empty. It felt almost chapel-like to Beth.

One of their father's eye sockets was visibly darkened with the commencement of the purple flush of bruising. A plaster had been placed across his forehead. He was very still, his breathing quiet, but Beth was relieved to detect the slight rise and fall of the bed sheets with each shallow breath he took.

'Hi.' Cassie's voice was tight, clipped.

'Hi, how is he?'

'He's injured his face.' Cassie motioned towards the bruising on their father's head. 'And he's banged up his knees. He fell forward trying to get out of bed and hit the bedside cabinet.'

Beth winced. 'But he's okay right?'

'Yes, he's okay. He was a bit shaken up, but the injuries are superficial, thankfully. He's had a sedative, so he's been asleep since then.'

Beth nodded; her eyes still fixed on her father. The familiar sound of their voices appeared to have roused him. James Hooper shifted painfully in the hospital bed. Discomfort washed over his face, as he stretched his limbs. His eyes flickered open, blinking repeatedly, even in the low light. Slowly he raised both hands to massage the loose skin of his face. He inadvertently nudged at the dressing and grimaced, as one hand trailed over the injury.

'Hello Dad.' Beth leant to kiss her father's cheek.

James Hooper hacked a rough cough to clear his throat. 'I'm so pleased you're here, love.'

A shadow of annoyance in Cassie's face. Beth pretended not to have noticed.

'Both of you I mean, of course,' James continued. 'Lovely to have my two girls here together.'

Maybe he had caught Cassie's look too.

Beth reached to hold her father's hand. His skin had become paper thin as the cancer had attacked his system. Translucent, she could make out the tracks of blood vessels and sinews beneath, could feel the hard outline of his bones against her own flesh. She smiled him, hoping it looked reassuring. Glancing up, Beth saw that Cassie was watching them both.

She might hate me, but she loves him, Beth thought.

'How's work love?'

'Busy Dad, you know. Tiring.'

'Oh, poor you,' Cassie interjected.

Beth looked back across at her sister. Was there a hint of sarcasm in those words? It certainly seemed that way. Her sister stared back, before quickly dropping her gaze. The look was long enough. Yes, Beth was sure she had seen a tiny flash, a momentary settling in of either hatred or jealousy. Maybe both. It was annoying, but then Cassie's attitude always was. Yet Beth knew the part she had played and felt the remorse anyway. Cassie had provided most of their father's care, and she had let that happen. It had made Beth's life easier just to step back and let Cassie take the lead, as ever. It showed too. Cassie was washed out, drained of energy. She even looked to have lost weight through her efforts.

Beth swallowed down the bitterness of the moment and said nothing of it. She turned her attentions back to their father. He looked so small in the hospital bed, like a vulnerable little boy. His slight body wracked with heavy phlegmy coughing. He wasn't going to hold on much longer. The bastard disease was getting the better of him. She hated it and herself for acknowledging it.

James had lapsed into silence, focused on drawing in ragged breaths. When he felt able to, he spoke again.

'I want you two to support each other, you'll need each other after I'm gone.'

'Dad I – ' Cassie interjected.

'No Cas love, we all know how this plays out. Let's not be stupid about it, eh? I'm dying and that's that.'

The two women looked across the bed at each other.

'And you Beth, all that stuff in the past, well... that's where it needs to stay. I don't want you back in that world, love. Promise me Beth? Promise to keep your distance? I know with your job that you still see those women from down there, but just keep it all at arm's length.'

'Dad come on. You know I've moved on from all of that. But if it makes you feel any better, then I promise. I am only involved on a professional level at the clinic, nothing more.'

She couldn't tell her father what was really going on, he didn't need that kind of stress, especially not now.

'Not from what I hear, love.'

Beth shot Cassie a hard look. Cassie just shrugged.

'Listen my love, I need to know you and Cassie will be okay. That you will both be safe and looking out for each other.'

'Okay Dad.'

Beth felt deep guilt. Such a bold-faced lie. She couldn't help it though. She was sure that Leah needed her. She'd been in her shoes. She understood what Leah was going through. Her father would never get it. The whole matter was abhorrent to him. What was the point of getting into some unnecessary heated debate that would only cause him added worry and upset them all?

'And Cassie, I want you to look out for your sister.'

'Don't I always Dad.' Cassie's voice was thick with bitterness. 'But I need help too sometimes, you know. It's not all about Beth and her life.'

'I know love. I want you both to take care of each other, right?'

The two daughters nodded their confirmation. The old man seemed satisfied and closed his eyes again.

Beth felt confined by it all. She was never very good with emotions and the wardroom felt tiny and overheated. She needed an excuse to step out.

'Cas, do you want a coffee or something?'

'Yes thanks, although make it a tea please.'

Cassie didn't bother to lift her eyes from their prone father and Beth was happy to avoid any further confrontation.

Out in the corridor Beth paused to lean against the wall. She drew in a breath. This whole situation was so damn hard. How did Cassie cope with it? She always seemed so strong. Beth by contrast felt inadequate and hopeless.

'Beth, hey Beth.'

It was Davidson and Bloom.

'Fucking hell,' she muttered to herself.

'Hello Beth, what are you doing here?' asked Abby Davidson as the two detectives approached her.

Beth gave them both a scathing look. 'Not that it's any of your business, but my Dad is in here. He's terminally ill. We don't know how much longer he has.'

The words caught in her throat and she turned her head away, not wishing them to see her upset.

'Oh right, yes of course. Look I'm really sorry about your father.'

Beth blinked back moisture. She was not about to give them the satisfaction of seeing any frailty from her.

'Thanks.'

They lapsed into an awkward silence. Finally, Beth looked over at Bloom.

'Brings back memories eh –' Beth ventured.

Bloom pursed his lips and nodded curtly before looking away.

'What is it with you two?' Abby was exasperated by the frosty and downright odd attitude between her boss and Beth. She was well used to Bloom's gruff demeanour and his brusque style with suspects, but there was something subtly different going on here.

Bloom and Beth exchanged glances.

'It's nothing Abby, just leave it.'

Whenever Bloom used her first name Davidson knew it had to be serious.

Beth rolled her eyes. She was so stressed and tired; she just didn't need them hassling her right now. She pressed her head back against the wall looking to the ceiling. The stretch in her neck felt good.

'You can say it, Bloom. The world won't end you know.'

Boom shot Beth a dark look. 'My world did end though, didn't it!' he barked.

Beth felt a heat rise in her cheeks. She could have kicked herself for being so insensitive. 'Yes, look Peter, I'm sorry, I know it did, I know. I didn't mean to come out like that. Sorry.'

Bloom sighed heavily and looked from one woman to the other. He made a pretence of straightening his shirt and tie. Eventually he addressed Abby. 'Some years back, Beth here, knew my daughter Daisy. They were good friends. Partners in crime might be more appropriate.'

Beth nodded her accord.

'And when I say crime, I mean they worked the Triangle together.'

Abby looked quizzical.

'The beat I mean, Abby.'

Davidson was surprised. She had thought of many possible scenarios to explain Bloom's attitude to Beth Hooper, but this one hadn't been in the frame.

'Oh right. You mean she was, that they both were...' Abby struggled a little to find the right words and decided to say it straight. 'Sex workers?'

Pain crumpled Bloom's face. 'Yes,' he croaked.

Abby opened her mouth to speak again, but Bloom raised a hand. 'No wait, let me finish. Beth will recall all of this of course but anyway... They were a wild pair back then. I couldn't control Daisy; she just did what she wanted to do and hang the consequences. They were into all sorts, weren't you?'

Beth just looked at him with sadness.

'But it was the heroin that did for my Daisy.'

'Daisy overdosed,' said Beth. 'I couldn't save her.'

'None of us could save her,' said Bloom bitterly. 'Some of us tried harder than others, though.'

'Peter, it wasn't my fault. I was a kid with my own addiction to deal with. I was hardly the best person to try to get her off it. What do you think I could have done? I was just as much of a mess as she was. You know that.'

Bloom's face crumbled. He turned to walk briskly away up the corridor. Pausing a few doorways away from the women he stood, head dropped, shoulders slumped.

'Peter, please,' said Beth.

Bloom turned and stared at her. A look of quiet despair. Then he trudged back to re-join them. 'Look, I'm sorry. I know you couldn't have stopped her doing the drugs. She was a law unto herself, my Daisy.'

'No, I'm sorry, I could have tried harder.'

Bloom waved Beth's appeasement away. 'I was being unfair. You were being dragged under too, I know that. You wouldn't have seen it like I did. If anyone's to blame it's me.'

'I think we both known it was Carl who got me and Daisy on that road. If there's any blame to lay it's all on Carl bloody Jacobs.'

'Yeah, he does have a lot to answer for, that's certain. That's why it worries me that you seem to have re-associated yourself with him, Beth.'

'No Peter, I haven't, not with him. It's one of the girls down there that's got my attention. I guess it's cos she's kinda like I was, well, like both Daisy and I were. She's the reason I've been back down the Triangle, nothing else. Carl has got her working for him. Says he's her boyfriend, but you and I both know what that means. I've been there and I hate to see the same pattern happening to this girl. I'm trying to be there for her, for when she feels ready to get out, get away from him like I did. Like Daisy couldn't.'

Abby stepped in. 'I understand how you are feeling Beth, but you do need to leave this to us now. It's a police matter and something that's best left in our hands. It's not safe for you to be down there at the moment, and I'm sorry to be blunt, but to be honest you're a hindrance. We are trying to investigate the murders there and we don't need this sort of distraction.'

'I haven't asked you to help me, have I? It's you two that keep following me, turning up wherever I bloody well go!'

Beth's patience had diminished as quickly as it had arrived. Davidson seemed to have returned to her usual form.

'And we will continue to question you if we need to. People have died Beth; this is a serious matter. By the way, one thing does interest me now. Why is it that you are here?'

Beth was incredulous at Abby's hard-faced approach. Did she have no regard for anyone's feelings?

'What do you mean 'here'? I told you, I'm here to see my father. He is dying, how much more do you need it spelling out for you?'

'I get that and you have my sympathies, really you do. This must be a very tough time for you and your family. No, that's not what I'm getting at. What I mean is here, working at the hospital, in the sexual health clinic. Why choose that as a job after your past? Surely that just keeps you tied to your former life in a way. I would have thought that you would want to disconnect yourself from all of that completely.'

Beth realised that people were always going to ask her this sort of question, or at least be thinking it. That didn't stop her feeling annoyed by it. Really, was she never to be allowed to just do her job without this intrusion into her past?

'I know this will sound very do-gooderish but I just wanted to put something back. I guess to help the women still in that lifestyle. Simple as that really.'

'I see, and you were never worried about bumping into 'old friends' down at the Triangle then?'

'Well no. When I started this job, I had no intention of ever going down there. The job is clinic based and as I am sure I have already made clear; I don't do outreach work. Really, believe me, there was no reason for me to go down there again.'

'But don't some of the staff you work with still do outreach work down there though?'

'Yeah, one or two, but I requested to be based here and I have yet to see any of the old girls I used to work with back in those times coming in here.'

'Hmm, and you weren't concerned about seeing Carl Jacobs?'

'Well no, because he never came in to the clinic. He certainly never used to come with me, back in the day. So no. I honestly didn't think I would ever need to see him again. I most certainly have not sought him out if that's what you are implying.'

'I'm not implying anything Beth, just asking a few questions to help my understanding of events.'

'Really? I don't see how this helps with your cases. It's nothing to do with them. Frankly, I find you're questioning quite personal and pointed.'

Davidson looked thoughtful, maybe she had finally grasped the fact that Beth was in no mood to get into this right now.

'Okay look, I realise we caught you at a difficult time. Maybe we can carry this forward another time.'

Beth just gave Davidson a hard stare. The police weren't going to get anything more from her, Beth was going to make sure of that.

Bloom moved to place a hand on Beth's wrist saying, 'We'll leave you to it, Beth.' He gave Abby a meaningful stare and she dropped her head in compliance.

'Thank you, and for the record Peter, I miss Daisy too.'

'I know you do Beth; I know.'

Beth's mobile buzzed the arrival of a text message. Taking this as a signal Davidson and Bloom turned and made their exit, leaving Beth to check her phone. It was Josh, wanting to see her later.

She hated how these 'little chats' with the police left her hanging, never quite sure what they were trying to get out of her. It always made her think the worst. That they most probably thought of her as a suspect for those murders.

The text from Josh had been a welcome break in the mood.

She tapped into her phone 'okay but come pick me up from my flat' and added her address. Beth momentarily wondered if she was being a little reckless in suggesting it. They barely knew each other, yet they seemed to have made some sort of connection. She shrugged off the doubt and hit send, before she headed off to find the nearest drinks machine.

CHAPTER 20

Having said her goodbyes to her father and sister, Beth's head buzzed with unwanted thoughts. She decided to avoid the human zoo of the bus, taking a taxi instead. Usually, she enjoyed bus journeys. It was an opportunity to zone out, drift. To pass the time listening to people's conversations and watching the world roll by.

Today, her head felt too full. She needed quiet to try to get it all in order. This coupled with a nagging need to be in the safety of her flat, meant splashing out on a cab worthwhile.

Her mind darted this way and that. Worries about her father's state of health fought with Bloom's words. The latter had the unwelcome effect of sparking old memories. The sort of thoughts that should say locked down tight.

*

Daisy had been her friend right from school. Daisy Bloom. Loads of the kids had taken the mickey out of her for that name but not Beth. Daisy had seemed so sorted, streetwise. Beth was fascinated by her, wanted to be her friend, be like her.

Back in those days she hadn't figured out that behind the bravado and the acting out, Daisy was already deeply damaged. She had been living a double life and Carl had already made his mark on her. Daisy called Carl her boyfriend. He was a few years older than the two of them, but she insisted that he didn't care that she was still at school. Daisy had preened a little as she told Beth how Carl thought her to be mature and intelligent for her age, how he said the age difference really didn't matter to him. Plus, he wasn't even 'that' much older than her. He was into the same stuff as the girls. Same music, films and TV and, unlike the boys at school, he looked after himself. Always looked and smelt good, wore the latest designer labels and celebrity fragrances.

Daisy had seemed smitten with him; said he had told her he was in love with her. She had smirked, telling Beth that Carl treated her like 'a woman'. When Beth asked what she meant, Daisy had nudged her and giggled.

'You know, Beth.' Daisy had been uncharacteristically coy. 'We've done it.'

They had collapsed into fits of laughter over that. Part embarrassed, part excited. When they had calmed down, Daisy went on to tell her how they shared everything. His smokes, drink, his money and his drugs. The mention of drugs was shocking. Intriguing, too. Her friend created an image of an exciting lifestyle. Glamorous even.

It seemed Carl often gave Daisy freebies. Her own booze and drugs, just for her. All he asked was for her to be friendly to a few of his mates when they all partied. Daisy had grimaced at that point saying that some of them weren't all that good looking and were pretty old. But it really wasn't so bad. Once she had downed a few drinks, or something from one of Carl's little plastic bags, it all became more bearable.

Beth could scarcely believe it when Daisy had told her, 'Carl really wants to meet you.'

It was an unexpected rush of excitement. Beth, being Beth, hadn't believed it at first. After all, he had Daisy. She was beautiful, amazing. Why would he want to know someone as plain and gauche as Beth?

'No Beth, he really wants to meet you, I've told him how awesome you are.'

Secretly flattered by the unexpected compliment, Beth said yes.

That is how it had all started.

She had never blamed Daisy for getting her into it. She loved her too much for that and anyway, she understood. Once she was into it herself, deep in the murk of it, she understood.

The blame was on Carl, all on Carl.

Beth recalled how, on that first evening, Carl had been charm itself. So naive she had been swept up by it all, fallen for it. Looking back now she felt such a fool. The trio had arranged to meet at the bottom field near to the girl's school. She recalled that it had been a warm evening so it had been a pleasure to be out of the house. Beth had dressed simply in a light summer dress, cardigan and sandals.

She was already regretting her choices, thinking the clothing must make her look like what she was, a young girl. Despite these misgivings she had felt an excited anticipation as Carl Jacobs had approached them. She had little experience of boys, let alone young men. It showed. She had been painfully shy. When Carl introduced himself, he softly took her hand to kiss it. Beth had thought she might explode, with the awkwardness of the situation.

Daisy had said, 'Right then, I've got someone I need to go meet.'

'What?' Beth had been thrown into panic. Daisy was leaving her here, with Carl?

'Yeah, don't worry Beth, I won't be long. Carl will keep you company.'

'It would be my pleasure.' Carl had shot her a warm smile.

'Laters.'

'Err okay, but don't be long yeah? See ya.'

Daisy had smiled and squeezed Beth's arm mouthing that she would 'be okay' before wandered off.

Beth was alone with Carl.

She could not have felt more self-conscious. Surely a mature man like him must see what an immature child she was. Anyway, why did someone of his age want to hang out with a kid like her?

He had been repeatedly glancing over at her, wearing a seemingly friendly grin. She had smiled back nervously worried that he could hear her heart pounding, smell the sweat that had started to prickle on the back of her neck and under her arms. She wished she had thought to freshen up as well as change her clothes before leaving the house. She had been in such a flap about meeting him, it had gone out of her head. Now here they were and she could barely think straight.

A little breeze had ruffled her hair. It had given Beth the chance to flick her head the other way for a moment and take a breath. Carl had also taken it as an opportunity and had reached out with one arm towards her. Beth had frozen, unsure just what he was intending to do. Carl moved a deft hand to lightly sweep a lock of her hair back into place. He pulled back his hand smoothly, to reach into his pocket. With a relaxed air, he retrieved a packet of cigarettes.

'Want one?'

She had looked at the proffered pack in his hand, feeling tempted. Daisy had smoked and some of their other friends had too. So far Beth had only managed to take the smoke into her mouth and puff it all back out in one great big cloud. She knew it must have been pretty evident to any smoker that she wasn't inhaling and that in itself looked uncool. She so wanted to look sophisticated and worldly in this moment. Best to not to take one.

'No thanks.'

Carl shrugged, had casually flicked the packet so that one cigarette popped up. Smoothly he pulled it out with his teeth, then light it. Beth knew that he had probably practiced this many times. Still, it was an impressive trick, to one so impressionable.

'Beth, I'm really glad we have a chance to talk. Daisy has told me so much about you. You truly are everything she said you were.'

Immediate paranoia. She had wondered what that could mean. Daisy was her friend, but she could be difficult at times. She had seen her jealousy of other girls at school before now. If Carl liked her, which of course she thought was highly unlikely when he had Daisy, then maybe her friend wasn't as happy as she had made out.

Crazy though, she had admonished herself. There was no way Carl could like her. She was a schoolgirl and yeah Daisy was too, but Daisy was 'experienced'. Beth felt herself heat up with embarrassment at the thought. She was an innocent, a virgin. What would Carl think? The thought of him knowing or suspecting her state of innocence was double embarrassing. But it was a fact, she still was.

'Yeah. Daisy is great, isn't she?' she said quickly.

Carl seemed to weigh this up, moving his head from side to side, his mouth twitching. 'Hmm true, she is, but then so are you, Beth.'

Beth had barked a short harsh laugh of disbelief.

'No really.' He had continued, 'I'm a great judge of character you know, I can tell that you, Beth Hooper, are a very good person.'

She looked down, letting long tendrils of her hair fall across her face, better to hide the redness of her cheeks.

Carl leant forward to peer round at her and beamed. She noticed how white and even his teeth were. 'I mean it. I reckon you're probably also strong, mature and you know your own mind. I like that.'

'You make me sound like a cheese or summat.'

Carl threw back his head. 'Hahahaha and you've also clearly got a good sense of humour. You got a lot going for you, girl.'

A smile had involuntarily spread itself across her face, allowing Carl to sit back in satisfaction. He had made in-roads with her.

'Listen do you fancy meeting up again sometime? I mean just you and me, not with Daisy.'

'Oh. Um, I dunno. I mean, what about Daisy? I thought you too were seeing each other?'

'Nah, we were but you know Daisy. She doesn't like to be tied down like that. She's got loads of other boyfriends now. She's off seeing one of them tonight, I think. So, me and her are just mates now you see. Honestly.'

Beth remained a little unsure. This was not the impression Daisy had given her at all. At the same time, she felt pleased that Carl said he was free. Even if she did remain surprised that he was at all interested in her.

She took a deep breath. 'Yeah then, okay I would like that. Thanks.'

'Great! And no need to thank me, pleasure is all mine, believe me.'

Carl reached into his pocket again. 'So how about that ciggy then?'

*

Beth remembered having been so flattered, so taken in by him. She had reached out and taken that cigarette with confidence. She had smoked it too and when she had coughed embarrassingly at its first light, Carl had not flinched. When she had blown out her big clouds of smoke, he hadn't batted an eyelid. Yes, he had known just how to handle her.

Oh yes. That was how it had all started.

Life had changed with some kind of insidious creep. A slow burn of adjustment. A gesture here, a request there, always building, until she knew nothing else. Carl's influence had seeped into her, taken her over, had gradually pushed her towards the beat. It had changed her. It was not that she had ever thought there was anything wrong with sex or wanting it. But Carl had gotten into her head and it became a battle in which she didn't want to lose face. After all, as he had kept telling her it was just about consenting adults. No-one was getting hurt. Any doubt she had about that, had been forced into submission.

Looking back, she wondered at how naive she had been. She was aware that there were some sex workers who had control, who only worked for themselves and didn't have drug habits to feed. The truth of her situation had been very different. The same could be said for many others like her down at the Triangle. Theirs had been an existence of control and subjugation.

Beth hated when her mind took her back there. Always too easy to return to those undesirable recollections. Always too vivid, still far too real.

Her last night on the beat had been a breaking point for her and that was its only saving grace.

She had rowed fiercely with Carl in the afternoon. She couldn't recall what about now. The usual stuff, most likely. Drugs, money or a punter. Whatever it had been, the result was that she had headed out on the beat alone. Usually, Carl would have dropped her off, returning through the evening to check on her. She had liked to tell herself that was the case. That he had her welfare at heart. The reality was that he came to take the earnings from her. For safe keeping he would say, in case she got robbed by a punter.

Yeah, right.

It meant she was perpetually on the back foot, always having to ask for her money back. Difficult at the best of times. On occasions Carl would make her beg for it. When she was rattling for the drugs she would as well. Dignity would be the least of her concerns. She would be down on her knees in front of him. Suffering his sneering as he lorded it over her. How pathetic she had felt.

Carl would crow about it. Laughing cruelly. When she reached the point of ragged tears, he would say he was only joking and not to be such a daft cow. He would causally throw a handful of notes at her, making sure she had to scrabble on the floor to collect them. He always seemed to take particular delight in the humiliation and power of the situation.

He never gave her back the full amount she had earned either. Overheads, he would tell her. He didn't take time out of his day to drive her to the beat for nothing. Or provide drugs free to her for that matter. He was insistent, she had to pay and Beth had felt powerless to fight back.

That very last night it had still been summer. A lovely warm evening as she set out alone. The sort where you want nothing more than to sit in a pub beer garden, sipping chilled drinks in the company of good friends. But Beth had a different sort of want. A need. She was rattling. She didn't much care if there was a pretty sunset or if it was a balmy evening. She just needed to get fixed up.

Carl was nowhere to be seen. Obviously avoiding her after their earlier row. She couldn't raise him on her mobile phone either. She arrived to find an empty street.

People could be downright off at the best at times. It had become common practice for folk to treat the Triangle like some kind of tourist attraction. They would come to gawp, as they drove by. Peering out at the girls from the safety of their cars. It was an annoyance.

This evening she heard the familiar thump of dance music. A car was approaching, and she could make out four figures inside.

Fucking great, bloody tourists, she thought. *I don't need this right now.*

The vehicle had slowed to a crawl in its approach. The driver pressed repeatedly on the car horn. Beth ignored them, looking the other way. The occupants all began gesturing, their arms flapping from the open windows. Were they so desperate for her attention? One of them shouted over the bass beat.

'Fucking whore! Dirty fucking whore!'

It was never pleasant to put up with this kind of verbal assault, however commonplace it had become. It may have become familiar, but that didn't stop it being unsettling. Yet whilst she didn't like it, Beth had become accustomed to this type of incident.

You had to make sure they didn't get a reaction from you. It only made matters worse.

The car turned the corner and disappeared out of sight. She sighed with relief but remained attentive. In the still of the evening air, she could still hear the music, faintly at first, then getting louder.

They had circled round.

Her heart sank as they approached again.

The driver slowed to a near stop alongside her. Something soft and wet was ejected from the window. Despite its apparent slightness, she felt the shock of its impact.

Whatever it was had landed on her skirt. Raucous laughter erupted from the car and the driver revved the engine hard before speeding off. The car disappeared once more around the corner. This time hopefully for good.

She carefully inspected the front of her skirt.

Saliva. That's all. Surely, she'd had worse things happen to her?

She fished for a tissue stashed in her bra. That was all, just a bit of saliva. Yet she felt sick. Her guts convulsing. She was well used to verbal abuse, but this? This was a whole different level. Somehow this just felt so degrading. Being spat on, like she was nothing. Like she was dirt. Fuck.

Looking back Beth wondered why she hadn't called it a night there and then.

The withdrawal had been in full flow though. She had desperately needed to make cash. Staving it off was all that had mattered. So, she had stayed out.

After the spitting incident it had turned out to be a quiet night. She had still been waiting for business an hour later.

But then, at last, a transit van.

She usually knew better than to get into a van but this one looked sort of familiar. Beth wasn't sure, was it one of her regulars, or maybe a workman from a nearby construction site.

One of them had been regularly stopping in his car and paying for her company in the last few weeks.

Still, this was a van though. All the girls said that you never get into a van.

Beth could see that there was only the driver in the front. Her nerves were jangling. Not only with the drug withdrawal. Her gut was telling her that something was wrong here. She was just doing her best to ignore it.

Squinting her eyes, she peered into the van again. It definitely looked to be just a single person. Beth felt a modicum of reassurance and clung to it. The van pulled to a stop beside her.

'Hiya.'

Beth leaned into the open side window. It was the same construction guy. It helped. She felt like she knew him, a little. He was middle aged, greying at the temples with the sort of tan you get from regularly working outdoors. When she'd done him in his car, he had always wanted a blowjob and had been quick to climax. It would at least get part of the money she needed tonight.

'How you doing this evening, love?'

'I'm good, mate. You looking for a bit of company then?'

'I most certainly am.' He was almost jovial in his manner.

Beth smiled politely, thinking 'Yeah, yeah, let's not have too much chat. I need to get this over and done so I can go get sorted'.

He might have been one of the better ones but he was still here paying for it. She opened the van door and climbed in. It was a temperate evening, yet as Beth climbed in the driver rolled up the van windows. She wasn't totally surprised, men often wanted that extra privacy, but they hadn't even started yet. He must have seen her fleeting expression, saying, 'It's the air con love, it doesn't work with the windows down.'

Beth nodded. She couldn't feel any cool breeze emanating from the vents in the dashboard. She would accept his explanation though, if it meant they actually got on with business.

Now in the vehicle she remembered his smell. The strong scent of aftershave partially covering an underlying odour of dirt and sweat. She'd definitely smelt worse. It was at least, bearable.

It was odd what stayed with you. Even after all this time the faintest waft of that aftershave on someone passing her in the street could have her retching, her stomach twisting into a queasy knot.

The van was open inside, with no divider between the cab and the rear. Beth took a moment to glance into the back. It was too gloomy to see properly, but it looked like there was a pile of decorator's sheets to one side. The strong blend of gloss paint and solvents competed with the driver's aftershave. She felt sure a headache was inevitable.

They had driven to a secluded dead-end street not far from her beat and Beth had set to it. Just another job. Get it over, the quicker to get fixed up.

He had already handed her the money. Beth lent into him, bending over his lap. His belt already undone, he had pulled his pants and jeans aside, giving her better access. Her nose was full of the stale smell of his genitals and she was keen to roll a condom on to him, creating a barrier between them.

Then, a sudden movement in the back of the van.

Instinctively Beth flung one arm behind he, scrabbling for the door handle, as she was jolted hard.

A blinding dizziness, as hard blows rained down on the back of her head. The driver raised one knee and pushed it upwards, forcefully into her face.

Two men.

There were two of them in there with her.

Two sets of hands grabbing at her, punching, slapping, groping. Two voices barking instructions at her.

'Get in the back now, bitch. Move!'

'Don't fucking speak. We are in charge. You'll do just what you're told or we'll cut you up. You got it?'

'We'll fucking kill you, dirty whore.'

The sudden aggression of the attack disorientated her. Was this really happening? It felt almost like she was watching another person going through the ordeal. Then the pain of the assault, the shock of it, would drag her abruptly back to reality.

The two men continued to punch and slap her as they maneuvered her. Between them they dragged and pushed her through the gap in the seats and into the back of the van. At first, she had tried resisting, but the attack had been relentless. Face down on the pile of stained rags, her head was forcibly pushed into them, strong fingers wound painfully into her hair.

The heady mix of paint fumes made Beth retch. Her arms had been twisted painfully behind her back preventing her from raising herself up away from the fetid rags. A knee was placed in the small of her back, as her skirt was pushed roughly up and her underwear was ripped down.

'No please –'

The men laughed at her. It was almost casual. The sort of laughter that you would hear amongst the general hubbub of conversation in a pub.

'Yeah, beg us bitch, go on fucking beg for it.'

'Please don't hurt me. Look, you can have it for free. Whatever you want, just don't hurt me.'

Hands gripped her tight around her neck, choking short her protestations.

'Shut the fuck up.' One of the men spat the words into her ear.

'We're gonna do what the fuck we like to you anyway. You're nothing but a filthy prossie, just another cunt, a worthless bitch. Bet you'll love it an all, like the slag you are. You will do just what we say, get it?'

Beth had no choice other than to nod awkwardly against the tight strangle hold and hope that they would get it over and done with quickly.

The memories of how they had taken turns to rape her were almost too much to face. She could never be quite sure how long it had gone on for. It had all been so disorientating. They had continued slapping her around the head, punching her in the back. Keeping her under control as they each took their turn. The violence of the assault forced her into awkwardly into the corner of the van, behind the driver's seat. Her head banged repeatedly against the metal side panel. The sound of it reverberated, even now.

When they had finally done with her, after what seemed a lifetime, they had dumped her out of the van. They had rolled her out. Left her lying in a heap on the kerb. Like they had just chucked out a bag of rubbish.

Well yeah, that had been made clear to her. She was just that. Garbage, a no-one, worthless. A thing to be used, in whatever way they wished. To be abused and discarded.

The only kindness, if you could call it one, was that they dumped her there, back at her beat. At least the bastards had done that. Otherwise, who knows when she would have been found.

She had lain taking in shallow painful breaths. Relishing the feeling of the hard pavement against the side of her face. Her only thought at that time was that she begged all the gods, the universe, whoever, that they would not return.

'Please, please, don't come back, don't come back, don't come back.'

She'd played the thought on repeat, trying to stay conscious in case of any further assault.

Eventually, it had been Harry that had found her. Driving past the end of the street at the finish of his shift. In the half-light, he had seen an odd-looking lump on the ground.

People often fly-tipped the Triangle, so he thought at first it was a bit of old carpet or some rubbish bags. But his instinct made him circle back for a better look. Good job he had too, Beth thought. She had a lot to thank Harry for.

She had been badly hurt by the rapists and her convalescence had taken some time. Whilst the physical wounds healed well, the mental scars were deep welts. The attack and the after effect had changed her life. In a very twisted way, the rape had aided her escape from the beat. Despite the horror of it, and the fact that, even now, she hadn't fully faced up to what had happened, it had been a catalyst. There was no way she could avoid acknowledging that.

CHAPTER 21

Beth had woken in a hospital bed, sore and traumatised by the rape. The Ward Sister and a younger nurse were in the room with her.

'Hello Beth, how are you feeling?' said the Sister.

'Bit sore.' It was as much as Beth could manage.

The senior nurse nodded. 'Let me get you something for that,' she said flicking back the curtain and leaving Beth's cubicle.

The younger nurse busied herself straightening the bedding.

Beth coughed and moved to sit up. The nurse reached to rearrange the pillows behind her. Beth tried to gulp. Her throat was dry. She reached for the plastic cup of water that had been left on the nightstand and took a long draft.

'Better?'

'Yes, thanks.'

'Good.'

'I wondered if I should tell the police. What do you think? Could you call them for me?' Beth ventured, inducing a further round of rough coughing.

The nurse paused in her pillow fluffing. 'Oh, well yes... I guess you could.'

'I've been assaulted.'

'Yes, of course. But aren't you worried about how that will look to them? With what you do, I mean.'

Incredulous. She hadn't expected to come up against that kind of attitude here.

'What, what exactly do you mean? Don't you understand, I have been raped,' she spluttered.

'Well, yes and please, I totally understand and I feel for you, honestly. It must have been horrendous for you. It's just that, well, they might not believe you. Because you work the street, I mean. Some might say that, because you're selling yourself, that it couldn't be that kind of assault. It not what I think, of course, but the police might. I've seen it before from them. It could be very traumatic for you. I'm just worried that you would come up against a really negative response if you did report it.'

'Looks like I'm coming up against one already,' Beth spat back.

She glared at the young nurse. Beth was angry but the nurse's words also made her feel like it could be her own fault. Was she making too much of it? Surely, she had the right to be treated like any other rape victim?

A queasy guilt sat heavily in her belly. Yet what had she to be guilty about? It had taken her enormous effort to shape the initial words. To say out loud that she had been attacked, only for the young nurse to reject her version. Maybe this was how it should be. Hadn't the men made it clear how worthless she was? That she was a non-entity, for them to use in whatever way they wished? If this was the reaction she got from a nurse, what hope did she have of getting the police to believe her? Perhaps this nurse was right and it would end in her feeling far worse, if that was possible.

She felt so dirty, so unwell and ill at ease with herself, it was hard to imagine she could feel worse. Right now, she would have gladly ripped away her skin, have gouged out her flesh where they had touched her.

The curtain twitched again and the senior nurse re-joined them. 'Here we go.' She handed Beth some medication and a glass of water. 'This should help ease things a little for you.'

Beth swallowed the pills, her eyes following the younger nurse who was rearranging items on the top of the bedside locker.

'Beth, I really think it would be worth you talking to the police about what's happened to you,' said the Sister.

The younger nurse glanced up, her cheeks flushing a little.

'No, I don't think I can,' Beth replied flatly.

'Are you sure?' continued the Sister. 'I realise what's happened must have been extremely traumatic for you, but I really think it would be a good idea to report it. You have clearly been the victim of a very serious assault.'

'No. Thanks, but no thanks. I don't want to talk about it with them.'

'Can I ask why not Beth?'

'Well let's face it, they are highly unlikely to believe me, are they? Who would believe the word of someone like me, eh?'

The Sister placed a comforting hand on Beth's arm. 'Beth, I'm sure they wouldn't see it like that. Just because you work the street does not mean someone has the right to attack you, or force themselves on you.'

'Yeah, like the police ever listen to people like me.'

She could see the younger nurse was biting her lip edgily.

The Ward Sister persisted. 'They might Beth. I'm not going to mince my words here, apart from the fact that you have clearly suffered a horrendous attack, you look unwell. I'm guessing there's some kind of drug in your system and that's made it difficult for us to medicate you beyond simple paracetamol. If you are willing to talk to me, I can help with that and we have links to a whole suite of services that could be of use to you right now. Just let us in Beth, please. Surely it's worth trying?'

With more of an exhalation than a response, she replied, 'No.'

'But Beth, I really think –'

Beth was firm. 'Thanks nurse, but I need to sleep some more right now.'

She knew she was being incredibly rude. The Sister was trying to help her, unlike her colleague. Begrudging as she was to admit it, the younger nurse was probably right. No one at the police would believe her. Why should they? Anyway, there was no way she could face going over it all again right now, especially not with the police. It would have been just her luck to get questioned by Daisy's Dad and he hated her, or wouldn't take her seriously.

The Sister had tutted, clearly frustrated. But she also seemed to know when she was onto a loser. With a shake of her head, she left the matter and Beth, alone.

Beth had snoozed a little although the pain of her injuries and the memories of last night seeped, unwanted into her dreams. Forced awake, perturbed, the urge to get out, away from the hospital consumed her. She could also feel the needs of her addiction worming their way in. Time to score, despite her incapacitation.

Painfully, she rose to a seated position on the edge of the bed and leaned to pull her clothing and other belongings from the bedside locker. Dizzy, she swayed a little, as she attempted to dress. The awkward slow reveal as she took off the hospital gown brought shock at the sight of her own naked skin. Bruising and bite marks tracing a raised reddened pattern across her body. Her inner thighs showed deep scratch marks. Her skin felt tender and there was burning pain between her legs. Looking at herself was almost unbearable. Like her body was somehow at fault for what had been done to it. She couldn't have hated her own flesh anymore at that point.

Of it all she didn't remember them using their teeth on her. Had she lost consciousness at points? She wasn't sure if it was worse knowing all that they had done to her, or being not. Beth shuddered and continued to dress herself as best she could.

She called for a nurse and the Sister appeared from behind the curtains.

'Yes Beth, how are you feeling? Do you need anything?'

'I want to discharge myself.'

'Oh, I'm not sure about that, Beth. I don't think that's such a good idea, you're still in need of a good deal of care.'

'Well, I am sure. Look, my injuries aren't that bad and I'm just taking up a bed someone else could use. I would be better convalescing at home.'

The Sister looked doubtful. 'I don't know Beth, you do have some concussion you know, we usually like to monitor a person when they have had a head injury and then there's the after effects of the attack. We can arrange for you to speak to someone, an expert in counselling rape victims.'

Beth's impatience grew. 'Look, I'm not interested. I'm leaving and that's that.'

The nurse sighed. 'Okay, I guess we can't force you to stay, although I seriously advise against it. I will go sort out the paperwork. Do you have someone at home that can look after you?

Beth nodded, keen to get moving. She turned to sort her belongings.

'Okay. Just wait here please, I'll be back in a few minutes.'

'Beth, love. Oh my word!'

The cubicle curtain swished once more and Beth looked up at the sound the familiar voice. Her father and sister stood at the end of the bed. Cassie muttered something to their father, too low for Beth to catch.

'Well, we are here now,' Beth's father said to her sister. 'Let's talk about it later.'

Rushing forward, Beth's father reached to embrace her. Beth winced as he pressed against her tender ribs.

'We came as soon as we could, love. Good God, what a state you have gotten in to. When we found out we were so worried, weren't we Cassie?'

Beth glanced at her sister. The look was returned coolly. 'Yes, Beth, what mess have you got yourself into now?'

'I'm fine.'

Her goal was to get out of here and score. Her family turning up had the potential of hampering that. She moved to position herself away from their direct gaze. The less they knew about her true state, the better.

'You don't look fine love, does she Cassie?'

'No Dad, she doesn't.'

'Well, I am.'

'I don't believe that's true, love.' Her father reached for her hand. 'Look, just stop a minute, please.'

She wanted to shrug him off but did as he bid. Her father was looking down at her hands clasped in his. There was a very visible series of finger sized bruises patterning her wrists, like mottled bracelets.

James Hoper's face creased into a landscape of pain and Beth felt guilty for causing him such worry.

'After you have spoken to the police, Cassie and I want you to come home with us.'

'I'm not going to report it, Dad.'

'What? Beth you must. Darling, look what they did to you. They can't be allowed to get away with it.'

Her eyes threatened to brim with tears and she forced her tongue to the roof of her mouth and blinked them away. 'Dad no, I don't want to. I just can't face it. Don't make me do it, please.'

Her father heaved a sigh. 'I really think you should. Look, let's get you home and we can call them from there.'

Beth opened her mouth to protest.

'I won't take no for an answer on this, Beth.'

She could see he was adamant. The thing was, they could all sit here arguing the toss over this, or they could get out of here and she could find a way to get away from them later. Best to give in. Then she could sneak out at some point, when the dust had settled.

'Okay, Dad.'

The tension in her father's frame visible loosened. 'Great. We have your room ready for you back at the house. It's just the way you used to like it.'

CHAPTER 22

The family home was set out on the rural edge of the city. Best of both worlds, Dad had always said. A few steps from the countryside, but easy access back to the shops and work, although Beth had found it too remote as she had entered her teenager years.

The house was positioned in an expansive characterful garden, set out with a small apple orchard, a vegetable patch and greenhouse. To three sides, the place was bordered by fields. It really was her father's retreat from the big bad world.

The view from Beth's old bedroom was just as she remembered it. The white dots of sheep undulated against the green, as the farmer and his dog drove them across the back field. So much time had been spent as a child staring out at that view, judging the seasons by the changing colours.

She sat on the end of her old bed. It seemed so tiny now. The whole room seemed somehow miniaturised. Dad had cleared some of her former life away. Her posters and ornaments had largely gone, but comfortingly the furniture remained in place. Same dresser and wardrobe, even the same flouncy lamp on the bedside table. To the right side of the room a door led into an en-suite, a luxury she recalled had impressed school friends when then they had called round.

With stiffened injuries, Beth rose painfully. She moved to stand at the window. The dresser and its seat stood to one side and Beth peered behind them. She smiled. Yes, it was all still there. As a child she had drawn little pictures on the wallpaper. Nothing very artistic, just random faces and animals, as well as written out song lyrics. She had hidden it all back then. Of course, now she knew that Dad had known about it all along and had indulged her. He had never questioned her about it, or tried to remove it and she was grateful for that. Seeing her childish handwriting and drawings gave her an odd sense of safety. It said home. Security.

She turned to see that Cassie had been silently watching her from the doorway.

'You okay, Beth? You look like you're in a lot of pain.'

'Yeah, I'm alright.'

Beth moved back to the bed. She knew the shaking had become uncontrollable and was now visible to her sister. To conceal the tremors, she pulled a folded-up blanket from the foot of the bed and wrapped it around herself. Cassie stepped into the room carrying a jug of water and a drinking glass. She set these down on the bedside table and felt around in the pocket of her cardigan.

'Beth? Really are you sure? Be honest with me, yeah?'

Beth again brushed it off. 'Yes, seriously I am. I've just got a bit of a cold coming on, I think.'

Their father had joined them and Cassie and James exchanged a meaningful look. Beth pretended not to have seen it.

'Or maybe it's flu.'

She continued, thinking this might sound more convincing. The last thing she needed was them knowing she was rattling.

'Of course, love, it must be,' Beth's father said, his tone placating.

Cassie drew two small white tablets from her cardigan pocket and proffered them to Beth.

'A couple of painkillers to take the edge of that flu. Here, take them.'

Beth opened up one hand, pushing it forward to allow Cassie to drop the pills on to her palm. A tremor made her arm jerk suddenly, as she grasped the medication.

Damn it, thought Beth but simply said, 'Thanks.'

She placed the pills on her tongue and took a swig of water from the glass Cassie now handed to her.

'Cheers.'

'Get some rest love, and we will come check on you later and see if you fancy anything to eat then. Okay?'

'Okay Dad, thanks.'

At least they hadn't mentioned calling the police again.

James kissed his daughter on the forehead and he and Cassie left the room, quietly closing the door. Beth crawled across the bed until her head reached the pillow. Dog-tired, she settled down. She only had time to wonder if the tablets had really been painkillers or something else, before sleep overpowered her.

Beth dreamed in lace. A half world, seen through a veil and filled with struggles. Unidentified assailants holding her and Daisy, pulling them further and further from each other. The sound of Carl's laughter echoing all around them. Her limbs being stretched out tightly. She could see her tendons pushing against her skin and thought she might be literally ripped apart.

She awoke with a start.

Breathing heavily and damp with her own sweat, it took her a moment to register where she was. She eased herself to a half sitting position in the bed.

Home. Real home. Dad's house.

That was good. Safe.

Physically she felt absolutely lousy. It wasn't just the aching from the rape and the beating. It was drug withdrawal too. That familiar unwanted cramping, the nausea, the sense of need.

She dragged herself out of the damp bed sheets and reached for the bedroom door.

Locked.

'What the hell?'

She rattled the door handle again in the hope that it was just stuck. This was an old house, full of odd angles and crooked lines. It could easily be a warped doorframe jamming the door.

Kneeling down, she peered into the keyhole. The metallic grey of a key sat snugly in the opening and a slight gap down the side of the door showed her that the lock's metal bolt was pushed firmly into place.

Damn it. How dare they lock her in. Was she to be their prisoner? This was totally unacceptable, even though they all knew what she would do if she had been free to leave. They had no bloody right to do this. No right at all!

The growing discomfort of withdrawal only fuelled her annoyance and Beth started hammering her fists furiously against the locked door.

'Dad, Dad can you hear me? Let me out of here right now! You have no right to treat me like this!'

She heard footsteps on the stair.

'Beth.'

It was Cassie.

'Fucking let me out of here, Cassie. You can't do this to me!'

'Beth, just calm down. You know I'm not going to do that. You're drugged up, anyone can see that. You need to detox, somewhere safe. So no, I'm not opening the door until Dad and I are sure you are clean of that muck. This is for your own good.'

Beth felt hot tears of outrage course down her face. 'Don't tell me to fucking calm down, you patronising cow. I am fucking calm. I'm unwell, that's all. Its bloody flu and I am not on something or drugged up as you put it!'

'Really? You don't sound it.'

Beth desperately wanted to kick down the door. It was probably all Cassie's idea. She would have quite happily punched her sister right now.

'Fucking let me out of here right now Cassie or you're gonna regret it.'

'Don't be so melodramatic Beth, and the answer is no. You are staying right where you are until you calm down and that drug is out of your system.'

Damn it. Beth could have screamed, but where would that get her? Not out of this room, that was for sure. She took a few deep breaths but sharp, abdominal cramps shot through her. Doubled over, the nausea returned. She really needed to get fixed up. It was the only thing that mattered right now.

Panting she said, 'Okay Cassie, you win. Listen, I am calmer now, honestly. You must be able to hear it in my voice, yeah? You can open the door now. Please.'

'I don't think so, Beth. You need to rest now. I'll check in on you later.'

'But Cassie –'

'I said no. That's an end to it. The longer you bitch and moan the longer you will be in there, so just go back to bed and accept that this is the best situation for you right now.'

Cassie's footsteps faded as she descended the carpeted stairs, Beth was left furious, frustrated and in need.

So many different types of pain pulled and pushed at her right now. Beth sank to her knees and sobbed. Angry, self-pitying tears but also born of the pain. Above her on the bedside table she could see the outline of two more of the small pale pills. Cassie or Dad must have been in when she had been out of it. Were these the same drug? If she couldn't physically leave the room at least she could drift away somewhere. It could at least help her to ride through some of the withdrawal symptoms. It was worth a try.

Trembling fingers reached up and she retrieved the white rounded tablets. She rolled them around between her pads, still unsure of whether to down them or not. A fresh bout of cramping and a strong urge to vomit made the decision for her. Beth swallowed the pills, helping them down with some water. She climbed awkwardly back on to the bed, pulled the duvet around herself, and waited for the numb embrace of the drugs.

The next few days were a confused blur, cut with moments of agonizing clarity. Long periods of blankness from the sedation helped. She frequently woke to find that her bedding had been changed when it had become drenched in her sweat or smeared in vomit.

Plates of sandwiches and fresh jugs of water were left for her, although the last thing she felt like doing was eating. She picked at the food a little, flushing much of it down the toilet in her little en-suite. If they thought she was getting better they might let her out.

Yet the door remained securely locked and no amount of pleading or threats seemed to make any difference to that.

During these days she could not recall hearing her father outside the bedroom door. She presumed he couldn't handle her distress. Maybe he would have given in to her demands. Or was it that he simply didn't know how to deal with the situation?

They had brought a small TV in to the room and a stack of books, the latter of which she devoured, happy to be transported away for a few hours into the tales and lives of fictional others. Plus, she could see out into the garden, watch the birds and squirrels feeding from the old wooden bird table her father had made many years ago. But the nights were worse. Maybe it was because she was so used to being out on the beat during those hours. Awake all night, working. Whatever it was, the withdrawal was always worse in the dark hours. Not just physically, but the mental hunger for the drug was so strong. She fantasied, making up elaborate unworkable plots to get herself out of that room.

If she had thought that first week was bad, the following weeks had been in some ways harder. The physical symptoms of the withdrawal abated quickly, yet coming to terms with how her mind needed the drug was a relentless challenge.

Cassie and her father had started to trust her a little more. They could see she was no longer sweating and shaking. They no longer heard her retching in the bathroom, moaning in fitful sleep or pacing angrily around her room. She could appear more like her old self to them, appear to be more in control again.

Inside her head though, Beth obsessed over ways to get out and get to a dealer.

A couple of times, given her new freedom, she had made her way to the edge of the city centre and hung at the boundary of the Triangle. But the memories of the attack sat like a hidden monster in the pit of her belly. They froze her with fear. They were probably the only thing that stopped her from going forward and seeking out her old dealers.

Back then, the hospital staff had all tried to get her to talk to the police, to no avail. Even when Cassie had tried to tease it out of her a number of times. Each round of questioning just made her shut down ever tighter. In those days of recovery, her father had eventually broached the subject with her but had quickly dropped the matter when she had become distressed.

She was relieved when it appeared her family had reluctantly accepted that she had no intent of reporting the attack to the police. Despite this there was an added weight of guilt to not speaking up. The thought that the rapists had probably attacked other girls only added to her sense of self hatred. But she had been so young back then. Still so emotionally and intellectually immature.

If she was honest with herself, she knew that the attack – she still struggled to use the word rape – wasn't the only thing that lingered. Her addiction had played a pivotal role in her need to work the beat. It had been a tough time and even now, years later she knew that she was still switched on to the drug. Being in the presence of it, of someone on it, made that old rattle resurface, just a little.

*

Beth pulled her mind back to the current day. She had spent so long trying to make a conscious effort to stop those days from defining her life. The truth was that it had all marked her deeply.

A distraction was needed to break this fogged mood.

The taxi had reached a point close to her street now. Decision made, she quickly tapped a text into her phone before leaning forward to speak to the driver

'Just drop me here please,' she said.

After today's stresses she wanted to call in to the corner shop before going back to the flat, to buy a bottle of wine, or a few. Drink, and plenty of it, was very much needed.

CHAPTER 23

The rasp of the intercom gave Beth a start, nudging the bottle she was opening. She quickly wiped up the small splatter of red wine that now dotted the table and moved to the hall. Still holding the damp cloth, she jabbed one finger against the speaker button.

'Yeah?'

A disconnected voice said, 'Hi, it's me, Josh.'

Beth pressed the entry button without responded, unlatched the flat door and returned to the kitchen.

She was already part way through glugging back her own glass and was pouring a second one for Josh, as he walked in.

'Hi.'

'Hi. Thanks for coming round. Did you lock the door after you?'

'Yes, I did. Nice place. Thanks for the invite, although I must say I was a little surprised to get your text. Pleased though, of course. How are you doing then? You look like you may have had a stressful day?' Josh nodded towards Beth's half empty glass.

'I've had better ones.'

'Really? Wanna talk about it.'

'You might regret that.' Beth was only half joking.

'No really, I'm a good listener. It is part of my job you know.'

She shot him a derisory look. 'Oh really, is that right? Am I to be another of your gutter press stories then?'

Josh looked horrified and jabbered, 'No Beth, no I'm sorry... I didn't mean that. Seriously, there's no way I'm that hard-faced or cynical. Honestly, I'm here cos you texted me and I was really happy to get that text. I wanted to see you. I'm not here cos of what juicy quote, or bit of info, I may or may not get out of you.'

Beth sighed. She really did want to believe Josh was genuine. For one thing, she needed someone's support right now. Secondly, she had to admit that despite her own judgement of the matter, she did sort of like him. It was hard to recall the last time she had allowed herself to be attracted to a man, let alone permit any kind of emotional connection like this. Of course, there had been others since the she got clean and left the beat. None of them had been allowed close to her, emotionally. There'd been sex with some of them. It had been a way for her to prove to herself she was over the attack. Yeah, look at me world, I can handle anything and still function like a normal human being. Truth was though, it was all front. There had been no triumph over adversity, no connections. The guard was always up, preventing herself from feeling anything towards them.

This growing friendship with Josh didn't feel the same. Something about it was thrilling, but immensely scary. Maybe that meant it was worth something. She just didn't know yet.

'It's my Dad,' she started.

Josh, true to his word, listened without interruption. Everything came out in a jumble. Fast guilt-ridden words. She had intended to just tell him about her father, but once she started, she didn't seem to be able to stop. Her difficult relationship with Cassie, more about her former life on the streets, the police harassment. She even vaguely alluded to the rape, although she couldn't quite bring herself to talk about any detail. When she had exhausted herself with it all, Josh wrapped his arms round her. A friendly, comforting hug. It felt good.

Gently breaking the embrace, they both reached for their wine glasses.

'Let's have something to eat, yeah?' Josh suggested.

Beth nodded. 'Okay, but let's eat here, I can't face going out. Plus, I have more wine.'

She smiled weakly. Josh grinned back.

Beth found two functional-looking white candles. She lit them and melted their bases, allowing her to mount them on a small, chipped side plate. They laughed at how unromantic the setting looked, but both took their seats at the kitchen table. Beth had brought her iPod dock into the kitchen and they enthused over their apparent shared musical taste. The wine certainly helped matters. Beth found herself to be at ease in his company.

Josh slugged back a mouthful of red wine. Emboldened he said, 'Thanks for tonight Beth, and for giving me the benefit of the doubt.'

'Huh?'

'You know... with what I do. My job, I mean. People don't trust us, you know.'

Beth raised her eyebrows in mock surprise.

'Yeah, yeah I know... you didn't trust me when we first met, but I really hope you now see that I am genuine. It meant a great deal to me that you felt able to tell me about working down at the Triangle. I felt kinda privileged that you were able to share that with me.' Josh paused and looked skyward, as if searching for the something, before continuing. 'God, I'm not good at saying stuff like this. I always end up sounding well cheesy. Okay, here goes... you may or may not have guessed it, but I really like you.'

Beth felt a flush of warmth and wondered if her face had reddened. He looked so earnest; she couldn't help but stifle a laugh. 'Well yes, it takes a lot for me to trust anyone with my background, let alone a journo, Josh. But I reckon I'm coming round to you.' She smiled. 'And I have enjoyed your company this evening.'

'Me too.'

She felt a sudden urge to touch him his arm. The air in the room seemed to have become denser somehow. Like an electric current had discharged around them. It made Beth nervous, self-conscious. She looked down studiously at her wine glass. Was it just her, or was Josh feeling it too?

Josh had picked up on her closed posture, taking it as the wrong kind of signal.

'Okay then, I guess it's getting late. I should get going.'

Damn it, thought Beth.

They stood, awkward with each other now. Beth walked him to the flat door.

'Okay then,' Josh said again. He opened his arms amiably, to offer a further hug.

Beth moved in to hold him. Her face was close to his neck and she breathed in the scent of his skin. The firmness of his muscles against her was a delicious thrill and she allowed herself a moment to enjoy it. Neither of them seemed in a hurry to release from their supposed causal goodbye, and Josh had raised a hand to smooth her hair. He let his hand wander down her spine to rest in the curved of her lower back. They both pulled back, just enough to be able to see each other. To be face-to-face. Almost instinctively she titled her head up to his and kissed him. She was relieved and pleased when he kissed back. Longed for flashes of heat rushed through her as he pushed her back against the door, the intensity of their embrace increasing.

Taking a moment to draw breath, Beth pushed her face into his hair.

'Stay,' she murmured.

CHAPTER 24

The clink of cutlery and the gentle chugging sound of a boiling kettle stirred her. Beth stretched in the empty bed, enjoying the moment. Maybe she was going to get breakfast in bed. She couldn't recall anyone else, other than family, doing that for her.

She quickly took the opportunity to visit the bathroom to pee, and to make herself look slightly less dishevelled. She didn't mind him seeing the morning her, she had no choice now, but at least she could try to look a combination of sleepy and vaguely alluring. She surprised herself, wanting to make such a good impression.

Returning to the bed, that still held its warmth, she settled back under the duvet. Josh entered carrying a tray laden with tea, toast, fruit and cereal.

'Morning gorgeous,' he grinned.

'Morning. Thanks, this is such a treat.'

'My pleasure. I hope you're okay with the food choices.'

'It all looks lovely.'

They both tucked in, enjoying the novelty of the shared breakfast. After eating, Josh took the tray back to the kitchen. He returned and climbed back onto the bed alongside her. Beth thought he looked a little thoughtful, distant even.

Oh yeah, she thought, *here comes the brush off.*

'Beth, you know when you had that funny turn on the bus?'

Beth was a little shocked, she couldn't remember discussing that with him. 'Er, yeah how do you know about that?'

'Cos, err, well, it was me Beth, that night on the bus. It was me who followed you back home. I'm so sorry. I never meant to frighten you. I know it must seem like I'm always saying sorry to you at the moment, I just keep fucking up, don't I?'

Beth recoiled. 'What the fuck? What the hell were you trying to do, freak me out? You scared the shit of out of me. What were you thinking? Jesus, was it you that spiked me in the pub? Was it some sort of twisted ploy all along to get me into bed, get a freebie? Were you going to follow me in to the flat and force me or something?'

Josh bolted up onto his knees on the bed. 'Absolutely not, Beth. Never, you've got to believe me,' he pleaded. 'I would never do anything like that. Seriously. I was trying to, in a very clumsy way I admit, but I was trying to protect you. It cuts me up to see that my stupidity has caused you to be so upset and afraid.'

'Oh really –'

'Yeah, honestly Beth, I totally was. Look, I wasn't anywhere near the bar you went to that night and I would never do anything so hideous as spiking someone's drink. I had been out with a couple of mates in town and I was on the bus you took. Pure coincidence, I promise you. But I saw you and you, well, you were kind of out of it. I mean I tried to talk to you but you were so vague. You didn't even answer me. Just stared blankly at me. I was really worried about you, so I decided to follow you when you got off at your stop.'

She dug back into her hazy memories of that night. There it was. She could now vaguely remember his hand on hers as she gripped the rail of the seat in front. Josh smiling down at her from the bus aisle, his mouth moving but the words a million miles away.

'So why fucking chase me down the street, for Christ sake?'

'Again, I'm so, so sorry Beth, you looked like you didn't know where you were. You were staggering along, looking panicked, so it kinda panicked me too. No excuse, but I stupidly started chasing you trying to catch you, I called out to you but you didn't seem to hear me. I can't apologies enough for the way I handled the situation, I just wanted to help you. I would never ever try to hurt you.'

163

Beth ran her fingertips back and forth across her lips anxiously. 'You've gotta understand, with my past, the way I was treated back then, something like that, someone doing that, well my first reaction no matter what state I'm in is to get the hell out of there.'

'I know, I see that now. I'm sorry, so very, very sorry.'

He had really killed the mood between them with this revelation. Beth felt like they had taken a good few steps back in what had been a brief, but telling, conversation.

'Okay, stop saying you're sorry, but please I need to know if I can really trust you or not.'

'You can, I absolutely mean it, you can.' He looked sincere and she wanted to believe him. It was true that he didn't know all the things that had happened in her past and how that had shaped her, despite her best efforts.

'Right then let's put this one down to experience and move on then?'

'Yes, please and thank you Beth.'

'For what?'

'For hearing me out, for not giving up on us, on whatever this is we have.'

'And what do we have?'

'I think it could be something real and I hope you feel so too, Beth. I think a great deal of you, you know, that right?'

Beth blushed, it seemed to have been a long time since a man had talked to her like this, if ever. It felt weird, she wasn't totally comfortable with it yet. Plus, his revelation had really unsettled her. But despite all that and how stupid he had been, she really did want to see where this was going between them.

'Let's just let it go, yeah? I can see how you thought you were trying to look out for me, clumsy as it was. Just don't ever do anything like that again, right?'

'Absolutely not. You have my word on that. Thank you, that sounds really good to me.'

'Right then, we both best get sorted for today, hadn't we?'

Josh nodded in agreement.

Beth rose from the bed and started gathering clean clothing for after her morning shower. Josh's mobile phone chirped the arrival of a call. He swooped to retrieve it before the caller had chance to ring off.

'Hi-yeah- what!? Okay, what are the details? Right, thanks I'll get on it.'

'Something important?' she asked.

'Just work,' Josh replied, still looking at his phone.

She nodded and headed to the bathroom,

After her shower Beth returned to the kitchen. Josh followed her in. He watched as she busied herself, putting the dirty breakfast dishes into a sink full of hot foamy water.

'Beth, can you just stop for a moment, I had another call when you were in the shower. I need to tell you something.'

She turned, drying her damp hands on a tea towel. Josh continued, 'It's Leah. I think she could be in trouble. One of my sources tells me there's a sex party planned for Saturday night and Leah is one of the girls.'

Beth's heart sank. 'When you say sex party do you mean a shit load of old men paying to screw a couple of young girls in any way they like?'

'I'm afraid that's probably exactly what it is. We need to tell the police.'

'That's not enough Josh, I need to go. Get Leah out myself. I can't just sit here knowing that's going on. The sort of stuff that goes on at those parties, the way the girls are abused, it's fucking sick. Believe me, I know. Give me the address, Josh.'

'I'm not letting you go to something like that alone, no way. I'm calling the police.'

Beth opened her mouth to protest again, but Josh continued, 'Hang on. They need to be told. But if you insist on going down there, then we are going together. Simple as that. There's no way I would let you do this without me.'

CHAPTER 25

'Thieving so-and-sos. You can't have anything of your own in this place.'

Abby was angrily muttering to herself in the work's kitchen. She opened and closed cupboard doors, roughly dragging their contents around in search of her personal mug. Clearly someone had taken it and used it. Maybe even broken it, knowing this clumsy lot. Whatever had happened, her mug was not where it should be. Had it at least been returned to the kitchen dirty, she would have been less annoyed. Not by much though.

Huffily she pulled out a random mug from one of the cupboards. It was grubby, off-white. Decidedly unappealing. Abby let the cupboard door slam shut hard, in irritation. It was either this or a trip to the cafe up the street. Abby was still weighing up the pros and cons of these options when Bloom popped his head around the room door.

'What's going on, Davidson? What's with all the slamming about?'

'It's nothing, Guv. Just making a cuppa, that's all. You want one?'

Bloom ignored her offer of a drink. 'Good, well in that case stop rummaging around in here and get yourself into the Briefing Room. We have matters to discuss.'

'The Triangle slayings?'

'Davidson, I know the press have been reporting them with that sort of sensationalist description, but please don't stoop to their level. But yes, it is about the murders.'

'Okay Guv, I'll be right there.'

'Now Davidson, now.'

'Yes Sir, sorry Sir.'

Abby happily placed the grotty cup on the work surface and followed Bloom across to the briefing room.

The room was already occupied by some of the other officers from their section, as well as a couple of young uniformed officers, who were seated near the front. Abby exchanged nods with a number of her colleagues and took a vacant seat to one side.

Bloom had moved to stand at the front. He was fiddling with the array of photographs and notes on the briefing room's board.

'Right then,' he started. 'I think it's time for us to have a little recap of events and discuss the results of the evidence testing.'

The officers in the room shifted in their seats expectantly.

'Okay, so we have the deaths of three mature males, all seemingly under questionable circumstances and all within the red-light district of the Triangle. The men in question are Derek Foster, Malcolm Smith and Nigel Franks.'

Bloom tapped his pen against a photo of each of the men that he had attached to the briefing board as he read out their names.

'Although the body of Derek Foster was the first to be officially reported to us, as a potential murder case, evidence suggests that Malcolm Smith was actually the first victim.'

'Malcolm Smith was a habitual drug user so it wasn't immediately evident that there was any foul play in relation to his demise,' Abby interjected by way of explanation to the other officers present.

'Yes, that's correct,' Bloom continued. 'However, it did subsequently become clear that there were a number of clear similarities between the three deaths and these have led us to conclude that not only were they linked, but that they were potentially perpetrated by the same assailant. So, in essence what we have are three deaths, drug overdoses, all caused by an injection of morphine, given via syringe to the left arm of each man. All of the men were of pensionable age and all frequented the red-light district to visit sex workers on what we believe to be a fairly regular basis. Malcolm Smith also bought his drugs from the Triangle.'

A few hands went up from the seated assembly and Bloom raised his own, palm forward, as if to fend off the potential questions.

'Just let me finish and then we can see if there are any questions. Now then, in case any of you were going to raise it, we are fairly confident that these were not cases of punters trying to improve on their sexual experiences by taking drugs with a prostitute. The evidence of struggle, the lack of evidence of sexual activity other than some initial disrobing of the victims, the positioning of the injection wounds and the backgrounds of the men all suggests to us that it's foul play here. Smith being a seasoned drug user.'

'Pickled more like,' one of the assembled officers quipped.

A brief round of laughter was halted by Bloom, who raised his voice and continued. 'Yes, yes very amusing, but as I was about to say, given Smith's history, he would have been more likely to have wanted to administer his own drugs. The other two men had no record of drug taking and their families suggest, no interest either. The drug used was high doses of morphine. A street drug yes, but still an unusual one. Davidson, we have forensic results that support the view that these were more than poorly timed misadventures with drugs, don't we?'

'We do, sir.' Abby rose and moved to stand at the front of the room next to Bloom. She picked up the paperwork on the lab results that Bloom had placed on the desk next to them both. 'Okay, so as the Guv has stated the deaths are considered to be linked. Forensics were done on all three assailant's bodies, clothing, their vehicles and any items found within them. These have established the victim's DNA in each case, but also the DNA of at least one other person. In the cases of Derek Foster and Nigel Franks both men were married, which has helped us identify matches for some of the unknown DNA we had found. Malcolm

Smith was not and there was only strong evidence of his DNA and that of one other person. This was cross referenced with other DNA found on Foster and Franks, and in their cars and there is a match for all three. Basically, what this means is that the same person was present in all three vehicles.'

Bloom stepped back in. 'We have also been fortunate enough to have found a syringe which was left, we believe by the assailant, in the car of Nigel Franks. This contained traces of Mr Franks blood and morphine, as well as carrying the same DNA of the person who we now believe to the unknown assailant on its surface. Forensics were also able to lift some fingerprints from the passenger doors of each cars. These are a little unclear in the case of Mr Franks but we do have good reason to believe they could belong to the same assailant and owner of the mystery DNA.'

'I would also point out the protein levels established from the fingerprint testing and the forensics from the DNA evidence collectively point to our unknown assailant being female,' Abby added.

'Well, that narrows it down then,' one of the uniformed officers spoke up. 'Doesn't that mean we are looking at it being one of the working girls? Not that it would be a surprise, of course. They are all dodgy as, after all.'

Bloom narrowed his eyes at the officer and gave him a withering look. 'Don't be so quick to jump to conclusions, lad. We need to investigate all possibilities here not just what might appear to be the most obvious solution.'

'Yes Sir, but who else could be though?'

'Look, I agree that the women working the Triangle have to be considered to be potential suspects, but we already have most of their fingerprints on file and we have yet to find a match. That's not to say that we have covered every sex worker on the beat down there. So, we do have some work to do, bringing people in for questioning and fingerprinting to allow us to exclude them from our enquiries.'

The young officer nodded his agreement.

'But,' Bloom continued, 'there may be others that we need to take into account. Family members, women linked to the Triangle in other ways, such as former prostitutes, drug runners, other criminals operating down there, or even charity workers. This could be about drugs deals gone wrong, particularly with the involvement of Malcolm Smith. Just because we can't, at this stage, prove whether or not these three men knew each other doesn't mean we can't discount the potential that they were familiar. It is still possible that there was some other link between them all.'

'Right then, does anyone have any further questions at this stage?' Abby asked.

The seated officers shook their heads, or mumbled in the negative.

'Good, well, we'll be assigning you all with a share of the interviews of the persons of interest, so let's all get out there and get on with catching this perpetrator, yeah?'

The officers started to chat noisily as they gathered up their paper and laptops before heading out of the briefing room. Bloom and Davidson hung back until they were the only ones left in the room.

Davidson studied her boss for a few moments, hesitant to ask the one question that hung between them. It had to be asked.

'Guv, the evidence of it being a female –'

'Yes, what of it?'

'Well, it's just that, well it kind of puts Beth Hooper in the frame as a potential suspect, in my view.'

'I don't think we can be in any way that definite about matters yet, Davidson.'

Abby was wary of his links to Beth. Bloom was such a hothead he could take it all the wrong way and dismiss Abby's genuine concerns. Phrasing her thoughts was proving to be less than easy.

'Sorry Guv, I don't mean to jump the gun, but there are large gaps in her story. Plus, her statement seems to change every time we speak to her. She has a number of times insisted that she doesn't spend any time at the Triangle, only for it to then become apparent that she does.'

'That still doesn't amount to evidence that she is the murderer, Davidson. It remains to be proven who that is.'

'Absolutely Guv, and I realise that if she were to be the assailant it may prove a little difficult for you, but I do think we need her to be on the list of possible suspects.'

Bloom rounded on her, defensive and huffing. 'It's got nothing to do with how I feel about things, or what impact this has on me Davidson. I don't want to hear you saying that sort of thing again, particularly not in the presence of any other officers. I would never be so unprofessional. This is about gathering the evidence and proper police work to find the culprit not just guess work. You understand?'

'Yes Sir. I'm sorry, Sir. No offence intended and I totally understand.'

Bloom's tone remained gruff. 'Good and for the record, Beth Hooper is already on the list and will remain there until we work out who has done these crimes.'

'Thanks Sir that's good to know.'

Bloom grunted and roughly gathered up the paperwork he had laid out on the table, pushing it haphazardly into a folder.

'Can I get you that coffee now, Guv? I'm nipping out for one,' Beth called after him as he exited the room.

A brusque shake of the head from the disappearing Bloom confirmed to Abby that she had probably overstepped over the line with him today. Still, when she thought about it, the fact was, that given any other case, her own attitude was the sort of approach Bloom would have taken himself. So maybe she didn't have anything to feel sorry about after all.

CHAPTER 26

It had been one of those mornings when time had seemed infinite in the clinic. There had been few visitors and the hours had dragged by. Beth had felt the need to visit her father at first light, whilst he slept and the ward was quiet. His small fragile frame had looked dwarfed by the hospital bed. The air in the room felt somehow altered. It even smelt different and she knew the end was coming soon for him.

Now in the clinic, with little to distract her, Beth fixated on the morning memory of her father. Her brain was stuck on a loop, replaying the image of him sleeping over and over. It was torturous. There was little she could do. Cassie had been trying to make arrangements to move him to a cancer hospice and Beth wondered if this was going to be feasible now. He seemed to have deteriorated so quickly.

This wouldn't do. This sitting about worrying wasn't helping. Dad wouldn't have liked it, she thought. He would have told her to get on with things and that life goes on for the living. Still, she couldn't shake the mood. She left her consulting room to see if there was anyone in the waiting room. It would be good to focus on someone else. If not, maybe she could ask her boss Jenny for an early finish.

There was only one person, seated with their back to her.

It was Leah.

'Hi Leah, how are you doing?'

Leah stood and approached Beth. The girl wore a heavy layer of foundation. Beneath it, Beth could make out the raised map of a rash of spots. These were frayed at their edges, allowing the makeup to catch and dry in tiny ragged lines. They looked like they had been irritated, picked at. Beth couldn't help but be fixated on the lesions. She wondered just how long Leah has been on the junk.

Leah spoke.

'Why did you leave me that day? With Carl, I mean. You wound him up and then just left me to deal with the state he was in.'

'Oh Leah, look I'm really sorry. I felt so bad for having to leave that day. What did he do, did he hurt you?' She reached out to the place her hand on the girl's forearm but Leah jerked away, shaking her off with a sneer.

'I'm fine, I can take care of myself.' Leah pulled at the lapels of her jacket, her head strutting.

'Well okay, but I am genuinely sorry. But I didn't know that you knew Carl, that you were, seeing him,' Beth lied.

'Yeah, well it's my business innit, and I don't need yours or anyone else's permission.'

'Yes, of course it is, totally Leah. Look, I'm not criticising or judging you. I just, well, as you now know, I kind of used to know Carl too, so I just wondered how you actually got to know him.'

'Why do you want to know? I don't see what business it is of yours. If you really want to know I'll tell you, but I want you tell me about you and Carl first.'

'Yes, okay that's fine with me. Well, we met because he went out with a friend of mine,' Beth replied quickly. She felt it might be best for Leah if she left out the other ways she and Carl had involved, for now. It didn't stop her feeling bad about it. More half-truths.

'That's not what he says about you. He said you were his girl back then.'

Beth sighed. Clearly Leah knew more than it had appeared. 'Okay, yes I was, years back. I reckon I was about your age when I was with Carl. But is such a long time ago.'

Leah looked smug for a moment, and then anger crept back into her face. 'So why didn't you tell me, Nurse?'

'Please Leah, like I've said call me Beth, and I was worried about what might happen if I did tell you.'

Leah feigned a look of puzzlement.

Beth continued 'Let's get real, we both know how Carl can be.'

Leah seemed to be somehow frustrated by this and started to pace in circles around the room. She was making Beth feel a little dizzy and anxious, yet she didn't feel like she could stop the girl. Abruptly, Leah halted to stare out of the window. Beth took it as a chance.

'Leah, how did you meet him? Come on, I will tell you more about me and Carl if you tell me your story.'

The girl's head dropped a little. She reached out to trace a line with one finger across the glass. Without turning she responded, her voice flat. 'It was not that long ago really, seems a long time, but it weren't. He used to come to the house sometimes, with my Dad after the pub. Dad would bring a few of his mates back to drink on, play cards and the like. Carl was one of em. Well, for a time he was, until me and him became friendly. Dad didn't like that.'

'Why didn't he like it?'

'I was still at school wasn't I. Dad may not have had much time for me, but when he noticed Carl kept making a point of talking to me when he was round, well he wasn't happy about it.'

'Cos he knew what Carl did, how he made his money?'

'Don't know what you mean.' Leah was quick to move to the defensive.

Damn it, thought Beth.

Maybe Leah had also lost her mother. She hadn't mentioned her yet, only her dad. Beth tried a different tack.

'Carl befriended me too, when I was lonely. Family life was hard for me. My mum died when I was still very small. So, it was just Dad and my sister, Cassie, for most of my life. You got any brothers or sisters, Leah?'

The girl shook her head.

'Bet that was even tougher then, if your Dad was busy, I mean.'

Leah shrugged and continued to stare out of the window. 'Dad made himself busy,' she said. 'He worked long hours and then it was down the pub, with his mates. He wasn't really interested in spending time with me. Carl was, though.'

'I bet that felt good as well, didn't it? Someone actually noticing you. Showing that they liked you, valued your company. So how did it play out, did you gradually start seeing more and more of Carl then?'

'Yeah.'

'And eventually you became his girlfriend?'

'Yeah.'

'Me too. Back then I mean.'

Beth didn't quite know how to broach the matter further. Leah seemed pretty sensitive to any probing questions, probably because of Carl's influence. But at the same time, she was here. She clearly wanted to talk, even if it appeared that she was struggling to do so.

'Can I tell you something Leah, about me and Carl, I mean?'

Again, the girl simply nodded. Beth continued.

'He got me in to drugs. We partied a lot and yes it was great at first, really exciting. He made me feel special, grown-up. I was just a kid really, knew nothing. Anyway, before I knew it that was my whole life and Carl, well after a while he wanted me to pay for the drugs, mine and his. He started asking me to spend time with his friends. Look after them, be nice to them he used to say. I'll be blunt, Leah. He made me have sex with them. For money, I mean.'

She could see that her words were having an impact, Leah had begun pulling at her own hair, twisting it round her fingers over and over in urgent strokes.

'Leah can you tell me, is that how it is for you too?'

There was a silence between them. The room felt oddly devoid of life, all activity momentarily suspended.

Finally, the girl nodded.

176

CHAPTER 27

A jagged dance of nerves pushed and pulled at Beth on the drive. Josh was taking them both through the gloomy city streets towards the Triangle. She felt like vomiting. The tension in the car was palpable. Josh kept casting sideways glances at Beth. She ignored him and impatiently tapped her feet in the foot well.

'We'll get there in time. Don't worry, we will get her out,' he said, reaching to squeeze her knee in reassurance.

Beth just nodded jerkily, pushing the nails of one hand between her teeth and stared out of the window. She watched the City as it passed by them. The same old streets, softened by the evening street lighting. People rushing home, or to nearby bars and restaurants. All going about their normal business, seemingly living normal lives.

Then there was Josh and herself. Driving through those shaded streets, to somewhere she really didn't want to have to go, to confront God knows what. All to try to help a girl that she barely knew.

It felt kind of unreal, scary.

They had to do this though. Leah needed them to. Whether she realised it or not. Otherwise, well... Beth knew how it could all end. She'd seen it before, seen it with Daisy. Girls so ground down, so broken by it all that, they gave up on life and let it take them under. Not everyone was strong enough to work the streets, or as fortunate as Beth had been to break away from them.

They had reached the Triangle now. The darkness always brought a change in the atmosphere of the place. Beth could see the shadowy figures of women waiting as cars passed them at a crawl. She shuddered recalling how she used to feel, doing the very same thing as these women.

There was definitely a more obvious police presence down here, which she didn't recall being the case back in her days. Probably a good thing, she concluded, despite her own recent run-ins with them. They were offering the women and local residents some sort of protection, simply by their presence. It had its limits of course. Evidently, they couldn't be everywhere. Those old man they had found and working girls were still getting attacked down here. Funny how the police had only gotten interested when the old men died. There had been numerous assaults on women down there over the years, without the same level of attention. Beth wondered how she managed to get herself sucked back into the place she had fought so hard to leave behind.

'Look we'll park over there,' said Josh. He manoeuvred the car into an unlit side-street.

'We'd best walk from here. It's not far though, just around the corner.'

'Yeah, I know,' Beth replied, as she climbed out of the car and quietly closed its door.

A sudden breeze tugged at her and Beth shivered, pulling her coat tighter. The uneasiness had not left her. It seemed to attune her to every tiny sight or sound, startled by them. It was ridiculous, she knew, and unhelpful being so on edge and she took in a few long low breaths, in an attempt to calm her hammer pulse rate.

Josh had walked on ahead. Beth hurriedly followed and they both turned into the next street. Harry was waiting silently for them. Harry held one finger to his lips and spoke softly.

'You took your time. Right then, it's up here, up ahead. Quietly though, we don't want to raise the alarm to soon. The police are on their way.'

The three of them set off walking in the direction Harry had indicated. They rounded another corner and there it was. A former pub long since abandoned and now derelict. The building had been left to rot, unloved, uncared for. It was unusually dark in this area. Street lighting had been permanently turned off as a result of local council's cost saving. It did nothing to calm Beth's nerves.

The decaying pub was a squat two-storey building, Devoid of charm. Even in this dim light they could see that its rendered exterior had weathered down to a dirty grey tone. The pub signs and its patrons had long gone. All the windows had been smashed at some point. Only jagged points of their glass remained, framed against a backdrop of rough wooden panels. At first glance the building appeared devoid of life, but as Beth's eyes became accustomed to the twilight, she spied barely perceptible slivers of light. She was unsure if it was the strain of trying to see, but they seemed to be flashing colours in slender lines, like tiny neon strips, bright against the dark of the window boards.

'How do we get in?' whispered Beth, pulling forward of the small group.

Harry grabbed her arm firmly, holding her back. 'We don't. We wait for the police.'

'But –'

'No!' Harry was firm. 'It's not safe, Beth. Lord knows who is in there or what sort of things are going on. Look round the side there. See how many cars there are? There's gonna be way too many people in there for me and Josh to handle.'

'Hang on a minute, Harry, I'm here as well, you know.'

'Yes love, I do know and that's my concern. These people have no respect for anyone, and definitely not for a woman. No, like I said, we wait for the police.'

Beth felt intolerably frustrated, but she hung back and fell silent.

The muffled sound of vehicle engines driving in their direction made the trio sink back against an adjacent wall. It was the police.

Driving slowly, a fleet of cars and vans pulled in, to position themselves around the old pub.

Beth spied Abby Davidson climbing out of one of the first cars.

Despite their efforts to merge into the gloom of their surroundings, Abby had evidently already spotted the trio. She raised a hand in acknowledgement, before quickly walking over to where the trio were standing.

'What a surprise. Fancy finding you lot here.' Abby's tone was sarcastic.

'Look, I know you're all keen to help. Commendable as that is, we need you to stay out of harm's way over here, right? This is a job best left to us, I don't want to see any of you anywhere near that building, you understand?'

Harry and Josh mumbled their agreement.

Abby looked intently at Beth

'That does means you as well, Beth.'

Beth reluctantly nodded.

Abby did not look to be completely satisfied, but with a final stern look, largely directed at Beth, she turned to walk back to join her colleagues. Josh called out softly to her, halting her progress, before stepping out into the road to join her. He leant in, close to Abby and spoke at a level inaudible to Beth and Harry, from their position. It was oddly unsettling for Beth seeing Josh and Abby in what appeared to be an intimate conversation. Beth was unsure why she should even care, but she did. Maybe it was something in the knowing manner Abby and Josh had with each other. Their body language hinting that this wasn't just a professional chat. Josh finished by placing a hand on Abby's arm and reaching in to kiss her on the cheek.

Beth was incredulous. What the hell had they been talking about that instigated such a farewell? It wasn't the first time she had seen them both together. They had talked outside the clinic, in the hospital car park. Seeing them together again, this time so at ease with each other, Beth couldn't help but feel confused.

Should she question everything that had built up between herself and Josh?

Beth quickly set her face in to a blank tableau, feigning ignorance, as Josh returned to stand with her and Harry.

Best to focus her energies on the police operation, which had begun to unfold before them. The police officers made various hand signals to each other and small groups of them huddled to speak in hushed tones. They quietly removed various pieces of what Beth took to be battering equipment from the vans and had moved in formation towards the pub. Eventually they all appeared to be in position around the building, ready to breach its doors.

Beth felt her heart might burst. It pounded at such a tempo; she was sure the others must be able to hear it. Josh reached out and squeezed her hand.

'This is it,' he whispered.

Suddenly the game escalated. The officers shouted commands to 'open up' through the closed pub doors, as they simultaneously hammered a battering ram against them. The doors gave easily. They crashed open, spilling a confusion of light, music and voices out on to the quiet street.

'Beth –'

Josh looked round but Beth was already well ahead of him. From across the road, he saw her quickly dart into the opened pub doorway.

'Damn it, Beth.' Exasperated, Josh followed her across the road and into the building.

The place may have no longer been a pub, but it had retained its layout with a series of small side rooms off the main bar area. The place had been stripped back of pub paraphernalia, but the large wooden bar remained, dominating the main space. On this stood a set of music speakers pumping out loud beats, amid a myriad of bottles, cans and ashtrays. Someone had rigged up an array of coloured flashing lights and Beth realised this was what she had spotted through the gaps in wood panels outside.

She was surprised to see there was even a tray of bar snacks. Was this just an ordinary party. Maybe a blues or squatters gathering after all? It could be that they had been misled about what was going on here.

Beth quickly stuck her head into a couple of the nearest side rooms. They were empty of people, although there was evidence of recent activities having taken place within. Both rooms had mattresses, discarded items of clothing and condom packets littering the floor. A tube of lubricant lay at the entrance to one room, squashed flat with a wet arc of its gel smeared across the carpet.

That confirmed it, this was no ordinary drugs or squat party.

The air inside the building was heady with the smell of bodies and skunk. Beth felt oppressed by it. The bass beat of the music throbbed and bounced off the walls adding to her discomfort.

She looked back into the main bar to see a trio of police officers scuffling with a half-dressed man. The three had managed to force the man to the ground, where he was now submitting to being handcuffed.

Beth crept past them intent on exploring more rooms. Away from the bright strobing glare of the main bar area, the lighting in the rest of the building appeared to be more subdued. Some rooms were lit with only red bulbs, others with strobes. A few remained in full darkness. This assisted Beth to pass unnoticed in the chaos that swirled around her.

Having silently made a full sweep of the ground floor she quickly progressed to the upper floor rooms. Someone had managed to turn off the music now. It was both a blessing and a curse, as she was now forced to move more cautiously in her search.

She crept from doorway to doorway, frequently looking over her shoulder. There was a need for speed now. It sounded like the police had also completed their searches downstairs and she could hear that more of them were heading upstairs to join the few officers already up there. It wouldn't be long before the police either stopped her searching or found Leah themselves.

The signs of the disturbed party were not confined to the ground floor rooms. Everywhere she went there seemed to be crumpled clothing, beer cans, and evidence of drug use and sex littering the floor. The upstairs rooms were all also furnished with mattresses, lain haphazardly on the floor. Other than the sounds of the police officers conducting their own searches, there appeared to be no other people up there with her.

Where the hell was Leah?

She reached the farthest end of the building and found a much smaller room. It looked to have been the pub landlord's bathroom in an earlier life. Beth peered carefully around the half open door.

Nothing. The room was empty.

She was just about to give up when a short metallic sound rang out. Stepping into the room Beth spotted what looked like an old airing cupboard in one corner. Tentatively, she opened the door.

There was Leah, squeezed in next to an old redundant boiler. Anyone larger than the girl wouldn't have had a chance of using this as a hiding place. Leah looked up at her, large staring eyes, glassy in the darkness of the cupboard, Beth wondered what she had taken to get her through the evening, or if the choice of intoxicants had not been hers. Had she been forced to consume a cocktail of drugs to make her more pliable, less likely to struggle and complain? That seemed highly likely given the nature of the party.

'Leah, thank God. Come on, we have to go.'

The girl rose awkwardly, squeezing out of her cupboard. She wore nothing but a cropped T-shirt. Her hair was tied up in a ponytail, but a few locks had worked their way free and the usually tight hairdo had given way to a more dishevelled appearance. Even in this light Beth could see bruises and scratch marks across the young woman's thighs.

Beth quickly took off her own coat and wrapped it around the girl's shoulders. There was the glisten of moisture on the girl's inner thighs and a darker smear that Beth could only take to be blood. Her stomach lurched and she hugged the girl. Leah stiffened in her arms.

'Come on, this way,' Beth said, her tone hushed.

She took the girl's hand, pulling Leah from the room. They could hear the voices of police in one of the other upper rooms, as well as that of one officer barking orders to the partygoers that they had managed to round up downstairs. Beth knew they had to act quickly. She silently signalled to Leah and they made their way quietly towards the building's fire escape door.

Beth pushed hard, it opened.

'Go on!'

She pushed Leah forward with a whispered hiss and quickly looked behind her. She was just in time to see Carl being led out of a side room by two uniformed officers. She must have missed his chosen hiding place by pure chance. He recoiled at the sight of her, but the police were already pulling at his arms, leading him away to the main stairwell and out of sight.

Beth exhaled hard and turned to follow Leah out on to the fire escape. The young woman had managed to pick up some company as she had waited for Beth. A uniformed officer was standing on the fire escape steps talking quietly to the girl. Leah had perched herself on the cold metal steps. Hunched up in Beth's coat, her knees were tucked tight up against her body.

'It's okay officer, she's with me. I'll look after her. Come on Leah, we can go back to my flat.' Beth was keen to get Leah away, as smoothly as possible.

'Just hold on there, miss. Who might you be?' the officer enquired.

Beth told him her name and tried to explain that she was a friend of Leah and she had found out that she was going to be at the party and so being worried, she had come here to see if she could help. It sounded terribly naïve, her delivery so gauche, that she was thankful for the gloom that hid her blushes. He seemed to be only half listening to her, partly distracted by the burble coming from his police radio. It didn't stop him being able to regard her with the cool air of a professional.

I bet he's heard all the versions people tell at these sorts of things a million times over, she thought, frustrated that she may not be coming across as genuine.

The officer allowed her to finish her account of events before saying, 'That may be all well and good miss, but all persons, including yourself, need to remain here until we have transport to the station. We need to question everyone present tonight.'

'Is that really necessary right now?' Beth gestured towards Leah. 'After all, she is a victim of what's gone on here, anyone can see that. She may need medical attention. Surely any questions can wait?'

'Yes, it most definitely is necessary Miss Hooper. We can get a doctor to check this young lady over, but you both need to come with me now down to the station. And we had best find this Josh of yours as well. He'll be needing to answer a few questions too.'

CHAPTER 28

It certainly wasn't joy that overcame Beth as Bloom and Davidson entered the small interview room. Someone had to take her statement of course, but she had hoped it would be some anonymous uniformed officer, so she could get this over and done with quickly. But no. Here they were again. No doubt bringing more of their probing personal questions. Like the bringers of her own personal Groundhog Day.

Bloom fiddled with the recording device, pressing buttons until he was satisfied with the set up. All the while Davidson sat, patiently watching her.

A belly full of butterflies, the staring competition with Abby wasn't doing anything to help Beth feel at ease. But then she guessed that was the point. Hopefully they couldn't tell, although Abby's smug look suggested otherwise.

Beth focused her own attention on the décor of the room. Bland grubby looking panelled walls, bad lighting and stained ceiling tiles. Why were these sorts of rooms always so dingy and austere? No windows, so no distraction or means of signalling. She had expected a two-way mirror, such a cliché of cop shows. Yet there wasn't one here. Just an uncared-for room. Not that it really mattered. She would say her piece and get out of here as fast as possible.

Finally, all seemed to be how Bloom wanted it and he signalled Davidson to begin the interview.

'Right then Beth, so once again we find that you have been down to the Triangle. I guess we shouldn't be too surprised given your track record, but then again, don't you agree that it's a little odd for us to see you back down there? After all your protestations, you turn up in the one place you were so adamant you didn't want to be. And didn't you tell us that you had no reasons to go down there? Yet here we are again after yet another visit. Plus, not only are you seen in the Triangle, but you turn up at a party organised by one Carl Jacobs. The very person you have stated repeatedly, that you are not in contact with at present, despite your past association. I am pretty sure you told us that you would have nothing further to do with Mr Jacobs. You see how this must look to us, I'm sure?'

'Yes, I can see that my motives may look a little unclear, when you put it in those terms, but you saw me outside with Josh Simpson and Harry Wood. Surely that made it obvious that I had arrived with them and wasn't involved in what was going on inside the pub.'

'Maybe. Or is it more the case you were all involved, and maybe you went outside to talk because it was too loud in there? Or maybe it was just you involved. You could have seen Mr Simpson and Mr Wood across the street and left the party to speak to them. Maybe invite them to join you inside?'

'No way! I arrived with them at that pub and that's the truth. I'm sure they will tell you the same. There was no way I was involved in that awful party. We went there to help one of the girls being used in there, not to join in.'

'Well, if that is the case, how did you find out about the party?'

'Josh. Mr Simpson had a tip off.'

'From who?'

'I don't know, he wouldn't tell. Said it was one of his sources and he needed to keep their identity a secret, to protect them. I'm sure you know how it is with journalists.'

'That's rather convenient, isn't it?'

'Possibly, but it's also the truth. Ask Josh, Mr Simpson, I'm sure he will tell the same thing.'

Bloom and Davidson exchanged a glance, before Davidson continued. 'So, do you want to explain to us who and how you thought you were helping?'

'Well Leah of course, Leah Robbins. Carl Jacobs has a hold over her. He's using her.' Beth turned her gaze to Bloom. 'Peter, you know what I mean. It's like it was with me and Daisy all over again. He tells her that he loves her, that she's special, the one, then he sells her to his mates or anyone who will to pay for sex. I had to do something, surely you of all people can understand that? If we hadn't got her out of that party God knows what could have happened to her.'

Davidson leant forward. 'You do realise that we had the situation under control, don't you Beth? What you did could have compromised the whole operation.'

'Yes, but it didn't, did it?'

'No, but that's not the point. It could have and you could have put a lot of people, including Leah and yourself, in much more danger. I've asked you before, but now I'm telling you. Step back from all of this and let us do our job. We are more than capable of dealing with Carl Jacobs and his associates. Understood?'

Leah was out now, so there was no need to be involved anymore. So, Beth felt happy to pull back from it all.

'Yes, fine with me, Leah in my main concern anyway.'

Bloom cleared his throat to speak. 'Let me give you a piece of advice, Beth. Stay away from the Triangle from now on. Events like this and the recent deaths down there, should be a clear indication to you that the area is simply not safe to be running around in like some kind of vigilante. You are also putting yourself in positions where we are having to repeatedly question you about what you have been doing down there. As DI Davidson has alluded to; it is hampering police investigations. If, as you insist, your motives for spending time in that area are indeed innocent, then you can see that your actions could be viewed as wasting police time. That is a serious chargeable matter and a distraction from what should be our real focus, catching whoever is involved in the deaths of those three men.'

Acid bile rose in her throat. Again, they had mentioned the murders. Every time they spoke to her, they managed to find a way to bring them up. How did they do it? They always made her feel so guilty, when she hadn't actually done anything wrong.

She must have been staring vacantly into space. Davidson snapped at her. 'Do you understand, Beth?'

She nodded and cleared her throat, to crack out a 'Yes.'

'Good. We are saying this for your own good, you know,' said Bloom.

Beth nodded weakly and feigned a feeble smile. It was all she could manage, but it seemed to satisfy them.

'Okay, please set out your full statement of the events, sign it and you'll be free to leave,' said Davidson.

Beth did as she was bid and was relieved to discover that they were true to their word.

Davidson silently escorted her back to the reception area. They had got what they wanted from her, no need for idle chat now. Leah and Josh were seated, waiting. They rose to embrace her.

'Where's Harry?' Beth asked.

'He's outside getting some air. I'll go tell him we are ready to call a taxi,' said Leah.

Once the young woman had left, Beth turned to Josh. 'Have you all been interviewed then?'

'Yeah, and all free to go, for now. I suggest we do leave, before they find something else to quiz us about.'

'Didn't they say much to you then? What did you tell them?'

'They asked me why I was there, and if I knew any of the people at the party.'

'And what did you say?'

'Well, I told them about my tip off and that we knew a girl who we thought was being forced to take part, against her will. Also, I said that we thought Carl Jacobs had set the whole thing up.'

'Thought it? We know it was him, Josh.'

'Yeah, but we can't prove that and anyway that's down to the police to pin it on him, isn't it?'

'I suppose so, but what about your source? Can't we get them to come forward, speak to the police? Surely that would corroborate what we just both said in there?'

Josh grimaced, 'Nah, there is no way she would do it.'

'Why the hell not?'

'Because she scared that's why. Look, it's another of Carl's girls, but there's not a cat in hells chance of her speaking to me again, let alone the police. She's gone off the radar. Can't blame her really, Carl Jacobs is one nasty piece of work.'

'Yeah, I understand that but shit, it doesn't help us at all does it. I just know that the police think I'm part of this somehow. The way they questioned me, they definitely think I'm still involved with Carl at the very least.'

'Nah, you sure about that? I reckon they will have questioned us all like that you know.'

'Christ Josh, I'm telling you I am a bloody prime suspect, the police think not only was I somehow involved in setting up and running that hideous party, but that I could have actually had something to do with the killing of those men!'

'Oh come on, that's a bit dramatic isn't it?'

'No, it's fucking not, and you know it's not. For fuck sake, they bloody well turn up everywhere I go, don't they? And they made damn sure they mentioned the murders again today. They want to know what I've been doing twenty-four hours a day and I just can't remember. I can't help the fact that I have memory gaps. Not that I've told them about that. That would just make matters worse. They would want to know why I have them and I don't know. But just because it happens to me, doesn't mean I'm off murdering people in those blank periods, for fuck sake.'

'Have you thought that the gaps might be some sort of PTSD type thing, or something related to that sort of after effect?'

'What? Do you mean post-traumatic stress disorder? Are you actually serious? Be realistic Josh, that's what people who have been through wars suffer. How could that be anything to do with me?'

'Yes, but I mean that maybe there's stuff from the past that you still need to face up to, like the assault.'

She shot him a look of derision. 'You know nothing of what happened to me then. Nothing.'

'No.' Josh spoke low and steadily. 'I don't, but I know that something really bad happened to you, you've intimated that much at least. The fact that you find it so hard to deal with it, is pretty clear to me. I'm just saying, it could be coming out in a different way.'

'Seriously Josh? Seriously you want to discuss this right now? Surely me getting a bit forgetful isn't the sort of thing that people get with PTSD? I thought it was all about reliving memories not blotting them out.'

'Well, I spoke to Dan, and before you get upset, I didn't mention you. But Dan, him being a nurse and all, said that loss of memory, gaps in time can be part of the stress caused by a seriously traumatic event. It's not just people who have been in war zones, although they probably get it full force. But symptoms of it can happen to anyone who has been subject to any kind of serious stressful or traumatic situation.'

Beth didn't like where this conversation was going. There was no way she wanted to talk about the rape, especially not right now, after the upset of yet another police interview. Yes, she could see he may well have a point about the losses of time she experienced. It did make sense that they could be related to the past, but she simply wasn't ready to face all of that at the moment.

Such a coward. Always doing her best to avoid getting into these types of discussion with anyone who had an inkling of what she had been subjected to. At some point she would have to tell him the truth of it all. Not now though, not today. Beth saw an opportunity to side-track Josh and took it.

'Right... Dan says so, meaning it must be right then, eh? Not like he's smart enough to put two and two together now is it? So, who else have you been talking to about this? Oh yeah, let's see now, there you were back at the Triangle having a proper little cosy chat with DI Davidson. Kinda looked like you've known each other for years or something. I mean fuck Josh, you even kissed her.'

'On the cheek,' he interjected.

'Yeah, and was that cos I was there watching? If I hadn't been there how would it have been, eh? Just what the fuck is going on Josh? Are you just with me to try to get information to pass on to your mate Abby?'

Josh shock his head, exasperated, but Beth was on a roll now, up in his face and ranting. 'I mean, are you fucking playing me here, just sweet talking me to get some good headlines out of it. I mean, Josh, how can I trust you when you do stuff like this?'

'Calm the fuck down, Beth.'

Josh grasped her firmly by the shoulders but she shrugged him off aggressively. 'Fuck off Josh, don't patronise me, I'm a victim here too and I don't appreciate not being taken seriously.'

Josh exhaled deeply and took a few paces away from her. Calmer now he said, 'Look Beth, I'll be honest with you. Yes, I do know Abby Davidson.'

Beth sniffed hard in annoyance and opened her mouth to speak.

Josh cut her off, before she had chance. 'But, it's not what you're thinking. Abby is with Dan. She's his girlfriend, not mine. Has been for a couple of years now. So, she's around the flat a lot and yeah, she's become a mate of mine, kinda. That's all there is to it, honest.'

Beth remained silent.

'And yeah, on occasions our professional roles have come into play, even conflict sometimes. Well, more than sometimes, if I'm honest. But the point is, I have never discussed you with Abby. I've said nothing about your life now, or your past and nor would I. I'm not about to do something that stupid and fuck up the good thing we have going. And for the record Beth, I absolutely do not think you are involved in those murders. Seriously, I don't.'

The reception doors opened again and Leah popped her head around. 'Come on then,' she said. 'Harry's sorted a cab for us all.'

The interruption from Leah had been timely. A welcome intervention that defused the moment.

'Okay,' Beth replied, happy to be able to change the subject. 'Let's go back to mine, get some take-out and stuff ourselves silly in front of some trash TV. Don't know about you two but I'm wiped out by today and starving too.'

CHAPTER 29

Beth blew into her cup of hot tea and sat down heavily in an armchair.

'Thank fuck we got you out of there,' she sighed.

Leah had squashed herself in the corner of the sofa. Knees up under her chin and surrounded by large cushions, she was barely visible. The girl hugged her shins and briefly glanced away from the TV screen. A small smile and nod were as much as she could muster.

Beth had to lend her some of her own clothes. A pair of jeans, a jumper and clean underwear. The clothing had swamped the girl's slight frame and Beth had found the need to pierce a new hole in one of her belts, to cinch in the jeans for Leah.

'I think you should stay here Leah, with me, for as long as you feel you need to. Would you like that?'

Leah rotated her head and flicked her eyes to Beth. Her cheeks coloured up and she looked almost embarrassed by the offer. If she didn't accept, then they would all be back at square one, but Leah said, 'Thanks. I don't know what I've done to deserve you, and Josh being so nice to me, but thanks, really.'

'You don't have to thank us.' Beth paused. It was great that Leah wanted to stay, but they really needed to talk about what had happened at the party, and what Leah had said to the detectives. Selfishly, Beth also wanted to know if her name had come up in the conversation. 'Leah, can I ask what happened in the police interview?'

Leah shuffled uncomfortably, pulling her legs tighter against her body. 'Nothing, what do you mean? I didn't say anything to them.'

Beth continued to press, keeping her tone gentle. 'No, don't worry, its fine. It's just that, they must have asked you about the party, what you were doing there and about Carl.'

'I guess.'

'So how did you answer them?'

'I told them that I was there as Carl's girlfriend.'

'Oh Leah, why did you do that? We all know that's not the true. I'm sorry to be blunt, but the fact is Carl doesn't care about you. He's only interested in selling you.'

Fat tears filled the girl's eyes. They spilt in small rivers down her flushed cheeks. Beth felt guilty for pushing so hard. 'I'm sorry. I don't want to upset you, but we need to know what was said and you need to acknowledge the truth of who Carl is.'

Leah nodded, sniffing and wiping her wet face against the back of her sleeve.

'I know,' she managed between sobs, 'I do, honestly, I know what he does and why he keeps me around. But if I had told the police the truth he would have come after me. He'd hurt me.'

Beth nodded knowing. 'I get it, I do, I've been there, remember? Okay, let's leave it for now, but we do need to talk this through properly later, yeah? Anyway, right now I think if you are gonna stay here then you will need some of your own stuff, don't you?'

Leah suddenly agitated, jerked upright in her seat. 'I'm not sure I'm ready to go back to my flat.'

'No, don't worry about that,' Beth reassured her. 'Josh has left his car here so I can drive over and get whatever you need. You don't need to move from here. Just relax. I'm happy to go alone. I need to go out anyway, to get some stuff from the shop, so I can just nip over there and be back within the hour. Give me a list of the sort of things you need.'

'Okay Beth, thanks but are you sure it's alright?'

'Yeah, it will be fine, no stress, I'll be back before you know it.'

Leah quickly scribbled down a number of items on a nearby notepad. Beth pocketed the list and the girl's flat keys.

'Be back soon then. Don't let anyone in that you don't know yeah?'

'Okay, cheers again Beth.'

*

When Beth reached Leah's street she parked at the end of the terrace and surveyed the road. It hadn't improved since her last visit. All the houses in the row had steps rising up to their stone-surrounded front doors, with small front gardens leading off the street. Most were overgrown and neglected. She could imagine that when the terrace had been built, the occupiers must have taken great pride in living here. But now the area was awash with cheap rentals, with many of the terraces having been subdivided into flats, bedsits and shared houses. It all added to a sense of transience in the street.

Scanning the street, Beth spotted a number of parked cars parked. Thankfully, none of them had been the one she had seen Leah getting into with Carl, that day at the Triangle. With a sigh of relief, she clambered out of Josh's car and headed towards the young woman's home.

*

Back at Beth's flat the intercom buzzed. Leah cautiously answered.

'H-hello?'

'Hi Leah. it's me, Josh.'

'Hiya Josh, come in.'

She pressed the entry button, returned the handset and hurried round to open the flat door. The friendly face of Josh appeared before her as he leaned in around the doorframe.

'Hey, how are you doing?'

'I'm good, thanks.'

'That's great.' Josh followed her into the living room. 'Where's Beth?'

'She went to my flat?'

'What?'

'She went to get some stuff for me.'

'Shit! You're kidding me? I really need to get round there then. Of all the times to have leant her my car, damn it.'

He pulled out his mobile and proceeded to search for a taxi firm number.

Leah blanched, her lower lip trembling.

'Oh god Josh, I'm really sorry, should I have stopped her?'

'It's okay Leah. It's not your fault. It's just that it's not safe out there. Carl could be out on bail by now. Or he could even have one of his mates watching your flat. I'm not trying to scare you Leah, but this is bloody worrying.'

Leah nodded vigorously. 'Yeah, I know what he can be like and I don't want anything happening to Beth either. I'm coming with you then.'

'Hmm, I don't think so.'

'No. I'm coming and you can't stop me.'

Josh could see the determination in the girl and knew it wasn't worth the argument. They really didn't have time to mess about. Beth could be in real trouble. 'Okay. Come on then.'

The cab firm had thankfully acted quickly to Josh's call and they didn't have long to wait for their taxi. In the cab Josh passed Leah his mobile phone. 'Here call the police. Davidson's number is in there and then ring Harry as well.'

Leah nodded and got to work on the phone calls.

CHAPTER 30

At the bedsit, Beth used the keys Leah gave her to open the main door of the house. With a quick look behind her, she stepped inside. The hallway of the terrace was gloomy with the only illumination being from a single bare, blackened lightbulb, hung from the ceiling. Ancient yellowed woodchip wallpaper clung grimly to the walls and she caught her heels as she walked across rough, greyed linoleum, that looked like it had probably been there for decades.

When she had visited Leah before she hadn't noticed how unsettling the communal hall in the house was. Maybe it was because she was seeing it in the evening light now and that heightened her senses. Or maybe it was just that she was concerned about who she might bump into there. Either way, it was far from being the advertised luxury conversion and Beth felt ill at ease in the shabby hallway. She walked quickly across to the front door to the bedsit.

The lock to the flat door opened with ease and she had the door handle down, when startled, she heard heavy footsteps thundered quickly down the stairs behind her.

It was Carl.

Before Beth had chance to draw breath, Carl was up hard against her. He roughly pushed her through the flat door and followed her inside. Beth fell heavily to the carpeted floor, her legs folded awkwardly beneath her. Slamming the door behind him, Carl towered over her.

'Hello Beth,' he snarled.

'Carl... what the fuck!' Beth gasped.

It was a struggle to get up on to her knees, but she managed to crawl far enough to put a little distance between them.

'No, please, don't get up,' Carl joked cruelly.

She tried her best to keep calm, to sound like the situation was all no big deal.

'Don't be daft, my knees won't take this floor, you know.'

'Ha! It's hardly the first time you've been on your knees in front of me, eh girl.'

'I guess not, but look Carl, I don't want any trouble, I'm just here to get a few things for Leah –'

'Ah Leah, yes now then let's talk about Leah. My Leah. What makes you think it's okay to take her from me? And what makes you think it's also okay to call the pigs to come and fucking ruin my party? You've cost me a lot of fucking money, never mind the damage that's done to my reputation. Just who the fuck do you imagine you are Beth, eh?'

Beth had managed to rise to standing now, but Carl had advanced towards her again, his bulk blocking her exit. She felt trapped by him in the small, claustrophobic room.

'Come on girly, give us an answer. I put a fuck of a lot of my own precious time, effort and money into that party and then, surprise, surprise the bleedin police turn up. At the same time as you and your hack boyfriend an all. Fucking odd that, ain't it? And then you have the nerve to take that stupid little tart away from me. Who the fuck do you think you are dealing with girl?'

'I think you need to calm down, Carl. None of us has done anything deliberately to you. The police knew about your little party anyway, we didn't need to tell them. I just wanted to make sure Leah was okay. She's just a kid Carl, you know she is. I had no intention of trying to stop the bloody party but there wasn't much me, Josh or Harry could do about the actions of the police, now was there? Seriously Carl, all I'm bothered about is Leah.'

'Why do you care about that dumb little bitch so much, eh? She's nowt to do with you. I've told you, she's my property and you'd best respect that.'

'I just do that's all, but I'm not trying to get between the two of you. Leah has told me you are her boyfriend. Me and her are just friends and I look out for my friends, that's all there is to it. Look Carl, I've had enough of this, I'm going.'

Beth made a dart for the door, pushing past him, hoping to catch him off balance.

'No fucking way!' Carl snarled, grabbing a handful of her hair. He yanked her head back and pushed her forcefully, trapping Beth against the wall, his full body weight pressing against her.

The tendons in her neck stretched painfully, as Beth's head was forced further back, and Carl tightened his hold on her hair. Her scalp stung with pain, and the pressure of his hold was blurring her vision. She felt little energy to resist and slumped against the wall.

It was all the opportunity Carl needed and with his free hand he quickly jabbed his fingers firmly into her neck, hitting hard at her windpipe. Beth felt like she could no longer breathe. As if her throat had closed up on her. Carl may have moved his hand away just as quickly as the initial jab, but the force of it felt as if his fingers remained, firmly wrapped around her neck. Like a choke hold. She strained, gasping, desperately trying to draw shallow bubbles of air into her contracting throat.

A harsh coughing attack left her nauseous and lightheaded, as Beth fought to stay on her feet. It was no good. The lack of oxygen in her lungs made her stumble and stagger against Carl. Still with a firm hold on her, he swiftly pushed one leg round to the front of her shins and pulled back. Once more, Beth crumpled to her knees. Carl sunk to the floor with her.

'Fucking bitches don't leave until I say they do. You need to be taught a fucking lesson, Beth. No one treats me, like that, no one.'

All Beth could do was to push out a strangled moan of fear.

Carl deftly pushed Beth to a prone position, straddling her. His strength and the speed of his movements took her by surprise and by the time she felt able to fight back he had flipped her face up and had her pinned, arms to her sides, his thighs clamped tightly around her torso.

'Don't you know me?' His face now up close in hers, words spitting air and saliva into her blinking eyes.

'Carl, please, you're hurting me –'

He laughed. 'Fucking hell, of course I am, you stupid bitch. I'll hurt you more too before you've learnt your fucking lesson. You're mine to do whatever I please with, until I tell you otherwise, got it?'

Despite her entrapment, or maybe because of it, Beth felt her temper rising. 'Screw you, Carl,' her voice no more than a croak from the pressure of his body upon her.

Carl's face darkened, his features a creased map of rage. She wondered how this would all end. He was looking wildly around them both, his hands tensing in and out of claw-like fists.

Searching for a weapon, she thought.

With a grunt of satisfaction, Carl reached out to the side to grab at an empty plastic carrier bag that had been partly pushed under the bed.

'Beth, you've always been a mouthy bitch. Never knew when the fuck to shut up, or know your place. Well, you've asked for this. You've only yourself to blame. I'll teach you not to fucking back-chat me.'

Carl sharply shook out the bag, before gripping in between both hands. He stretched it out in front of her and time seemed to stand still. He was grinning widely, a manic look in his eyes. Then, Carl firmly pushed the carrier bag over Beth's face, pressing down.

The bag quickly pulled tight around her head, blinding Beth, filling her nose and mouth, as she uncontrollably drew in a sharp breath. This simply allowed Carl to press harder, pulling the bag closer to the sides of her head.

Beth gagged. She struggled ineffectually against his hold on her. Adrenaline was flooding through her. Even now, 'the nurse' in her mind raced through thoughts of what the lack of air was doing to her body. She imagined the slowing down of the movement of oxygen molecules in her blood, leaving her brain deprived. Soon she would become confused, maybe even euphoric before she passed out.

She was still with it enough to hear him, even if it was muffled by the bag and his fists pressed against her ears. He was ranting and moaning with the excursions of her suffocation.

'Fucking bitch, fucking dumb little bitch. No whore betters me, especially not a nobody like you. I'll show you who the fucking boss is, you fucking interfering bitch.'

If. I can only-hang on, thought Beth.

She tried to stay in the moment, but the pounding of her own blood filled her ears. Suddenly, she felt very light and calm. The pressure was lifted from her body. It felt like the bag was being pulled from her face.

She started to let go.

This is I, she thought. *I'm dying, I must be. This must be the embrace of it.*

'Beth! Beth love, wake up, can you hear me, Beth? Come on Beth, stay with us. Wake up, come back to us.'

Rough shaking and a series of sharp slaps to her face accompanied by an urgent voice pushed their way into her slipping world. With difficulty Beth opened her eyes, to see blurred, but concerned faces above her.

'Thank God,' said a disconnected voice. 'You had us worried there, love.'

CHAPTER 31

An appropriate bleakness had settled into the morning's weather. Beth had a dull headache and the undulations of nausea. Her mood was sombre, as was befitting the upcoming events.

Her father's funeral had seemed insensitively long off when he had first died. Yet here it was, forcing itself upon her. She stared out of the living room window, watching the wind push shrouded folds of mist across the garden and drag at leaves on the bowing trees.

Funny how childhood memories always seemed to be clad in summer colours. She saw herself clambering up through green foliage. Cassie always below her, stressing, as she climbed higher and higher in a favourite apple tree. Her sister would pace around the trunk, staring up at her with her hands on her hips until Beth, having stuffed her pockets with ripening fruit, would grow weary of the game and descend to the lawn below. Cassie would chastise her, but they would carry the fruit into the kitchen together, where her sister would teach her to bake apple pie or crush their pulp into fresh apple juice. It all seemed ridiculously idyllic now.

A hand gently cupped her shoulder. It was Josh. She smiled weakly at him and he leant to wrap his arms around her. She leant back into him, glad of the closeness.

'Okay love, you know it's time, yeah?' His tone soft. 'You ready to go? Cassie is waiting for us outside.'

Beth sighed heavily. It wasn't just the funeral that filled her with such a weight. Having to deal with all the other people who would attend was what she feared the most. Selfish she knew, but trying to handle their grief, on top of her own cavernous loss, was daunting. At least she had Josh, and Cassie. They could all support each other to get through the day, she hoped.

Cassie was already seated out in the funeral car. Beth glanced at the hearse at the front. The sight of the coffin, bedecked with flowers, knowing that her father's body was inside, caused her headache to hammer a little harder. The knot in her gut tightened a little more. She quickly climbed into the car next to her sister. Cassie moved over a little, to let her fasten her seatbelt, before reaching her hand to hold Beth's.

The journey to the chapel passed in silence.

It felt surreal to Beth when they entered the church. She wasn't sure what she expected. It wasn't as if she hadn't been to a funeral before. But this was her father's funeral. This was Dad. Lying in that wooden box. It was like some kind of horrible dream. The rows of attendees became one indistinct mass of faces to her, as she moved forward. Relieved, she found her seat, no longer the focus of all those sympathetic eyes.

There had been songs, she knew that much, and readings. But the service was a blur to Beth. Her senses seemed both heightened and dulled by grief at the same time. It didn't make sense, but then when did death ever make sense, Beth thought. She found it best to focus on the decorations on top of her father's coffin. It had carried an array of colourful flowers and a carefully chosen photo of James Hooper. Her father's face smiled at her from the picture and she again found it hard to see the events of the day as reality.

When the service was over, she and Cassie moved to stand at the exit doors, greeting the mourners who filed past them. A parade of kind words, handshakes and hugs. Almost too much to bear.

Cassie had insisted on a burial and this meant the ceremony was to continue by the graveside.

Beth had walked through the graveyard quite regularly and had always found it to be a calming place. Yet today, the dull aching reason for their presence and the dour weather made her feel rightly ill at ease.

The majority of the mourners had left, setting off for the wake, which was being held back at her father's house, but the two sisters and Josh stood by the graveside. The wind had picked up, whipping around their legs and stealing the words from the vicar's mouth, as they said their final goodbyes.

The trio stood in an embrace. Beth welcomed the warmth of it, looking out across the graveyard. She watched the vicar walk respectfully away. They were finally left to their contemplation, or so she thought. Cassie and Josh were huddled against the chill, still looking down into the grave, but Beth had continued to survey the cemetery. She spied two figures, standing side by side under a small group of trees some metres away.

It was Bloom and Davidson.

'What the fuck? Have they no respect, how dare they turn up here today?' she exploded.

Cassie and Josh turned to look in the direction of Beth's anger. The detectives had clearly noticed that they had been spotted, yet they lingered, silently under the tree canopy.

'They have no right to be here. How insensitive can they be? I'm going to bloody well give them a piece of my mind,' said Beth angrily.

Cassie reached a hand to stop her. 'No Beth, let me go.'

'But –'

'No. I said I will go. It's better if I speak to them. You make your way back to the car please.'

Cassie turned to Josh. 'Make sure she gets into the car, please.'

Josh nodded placing an arm protectively around Beth. 'Come on love, don't let them upset you, just leave it to Cassie, yeah?'

Beth was furious at the intrusion of the police into their grief, but she knew they were both right. Cassie would handle the situation much more calmly than she could.

Indignant, Beth sat fuming in the car, waiting for her sister to finish talking to the detectives. Eventually Cassie climbed into the car beside her, leaving the police officers to remain, in their lurking position under the tree line.

'What did they want then? The bold-faced nerve of them turning up today, so insensitive.' Beth felt almost desperate to know why they had attended.

'Nothing, don't worry. It's not important.'

'It can't have been nothing, never is with those two. Did they want to ask you about me?'

Cassie turned to her, anger writ across her face. 'Look Beth, just drop it. It wasn't about you. Guess what, not everything is focused on you. They just wanted to pay their respects to Dad. That's all.'

Beth didn't believe that for one moment. Bloom may have known their father when she was young, but that was only because of the trouble she and Daisy had gotten into. No, there was no way they were there just there for Dad.

She opened her mouth to speak again but Cassie had turned away from her and was pointedly staring out of the window. Silence reigned once more as they made the journey back to their father's house.

CHAPTER 32

Back at the family home, all the rarely seen relatives, do-gooders and neighbours had departed, leaving a hollow air to settle across the rooms. Cassie broke the mood, bustling about, clearing up. Putting the house back into order, she called it.

There hadn't been any further opportunities for Beth to question her sister about the graveyard conversation with the police. The day had been full on with the supposed well-wishers who had turned up at the house. She felt bad for thinking the worst of these people. After all, they had been good enough to make the effort to attend. Still, embroiled in her own anger and guilt, Beth could not help but doubt the intent of others.

They had all spoken so highly of her father. Had expressed to the sisters what a gentleman he had been. Said how brave of him to raise two daughters alone for all those years. Yet they all stopped short of saying what a credit she and Cassie were to him, and she knew why. It didn't matter with some people how distanced you were from the supposed wrong things you had done. They would still find a way to look down on you. It was a fact of life, thought Beth, there are just some very judgmental types out there, who would always think that way about her. She was big enough to rise above it though. Or too stubborn to let them get to her.

Not fair on Cassie, though. She looked across at her sister who was still busily gathering up dirty plates and napkins. Cassie had always been the good one. The rational, sensible sister. They had no right to tar her with the same brush as they used for Beth.

Cassie must have felt her gaze and raised her eyes to meet Beth's. A small smile twitched across her face. making the skin around her eyes crinkle. She moved to turn on Dad's old CD player which stood on the nearby sideboard. It started playing some old Rolling Stones album, one of Dad's, *Sticky Fingers* she thought it was called. It was a memorable album. Not for the music so much as for the record sleeve artwork. It had been of much interest to her as a young girl, with its image of a man's crotch and a working zip in the jeans he was wearing. The music had never been quite her taste though, and she was surprised that it seemed that Cassie liked it.

'You going to keep Dad's music then?'

Beth looked quizzically across at her sister and handed Josh the full bin liner she held. 'Take that to the bin for us would you, please?'

'Sure thing,' he replied, exiting the room.

Cassie was standing swaying to the music, her arms crossed over her chest. She had her eyes half closed and her hair had fallen down, concealing part of her face.

'The Stones were never your thing were they, Beth?' Cassie had a strange flat tone to her voice.

'I guess not.'

'No, you always seemed to enjoy the darker stuff. All that miserable goth stuff you used to wallow in. Do you remember when you found Dad's Velvet Underground collection? You played that stuff over and over, non-stop. Drove me mad. Even Dad got fed up with it and they were his albums.'

Beth nodded.

'Yeah, that was more your thing.'

'Yeah, it's true. I still like that stuff as well, although I like to think I've broadened out in my musical taste these days,' said Beth.

Cassie nodded to herself. 'Do you think music can influence who we become, how we evolve as people?'

Beth was a little puzzled. Just where was her sister going with this, she wondered? She shrugged.

'I mean, well, it affects you emotionally, brings out parts of you that are hidden, that you maybe didn't even know existed, but that are still aspects of who you are. Don't you think?' continued Cassie.

'Hmm, yeah maybe. I don't really understand what you're getting at though Cas. What is it you're trying to say here?'

'Well, I had been thinking about that one Velvet Underground song you used play so much. That one with the awful drug name. Heroin, wasn't it?'

Oh, now I fucking see. So that's where this is going. Same old fucking story, thought Beth with annoyance.

'Really Cassie? You want to go there today, of all fucking days?'

'No wait Beth, I'm sorry it's not about your past. No, it's not that at all. Just hear me out. I'm not trying to get at you. Really. I'm not. I, well I need to tell you something.'

'Okay then, go on, I'm all ears.' Beth perched herself on the edge of the sofa and clapped her hands down on to her knees. 'Well, go on, what is it?'

Cassie started to pace back and forth across the room. She clenched and unclenched her hands a number of times, her mouth twisting into wordless shapes.

'Come on Cas, spit it out? What is it you're trying to say to me? God, after today it surely can't be anything that bad.'

This seemed to have had the right affect. Cassie halted her pacing and swiftly turned to face Beth. She blurted, 'When you were on the drugs and working the streets –'

'Fucking hell, Cassie, I thought you said you weren't going to have a fucking go. You know how hard all that was for me, how difficult it was to get clean and stay that way. Why do you want to go there now, today?'

'Beth, please I'm not. Please just let me finish. I have to get this out now. There's no other time. I need to say this to you.'

Beth felt annoyed and more than a little confused, but she held her hands up and gestured for her sister to continue.

'When Dad and I helped you get out of that awful mess, well the truth is I was jealous.'

Beth looked at her sister, incredulous at her words. 'Of what, for fuck sake? Christ, my life was one long nightmare of shit back then. Believe me you had nothing to be jealous of.'

'Yes, I know how very tough it all was for you. But in a way, for me, and maybe because of how tough it was, it felt like all the attention, Dad's attention, was focused on you. I know that must sound selfish and you will think me silly, but it all seemed to have a kind of tawdry glamour to it, you know?'

'I can assure you there was nothing glamorous about working the beat or prostituting yourself anywhere else, in my view. Sex work is far from being my best move and you know how it was, how I was coerced into it by Carl. I didn't choose to live that life, it chose me.'

'Yes of course I know that, believe me, I do really know that now.'

'What do you mean, now? Surely you knew it back then. You saw how I was, what a state I ended up in. Why has it taken you until now to cotton on to how destructive that sort of lifestyle is? I mean, good god, the number of times I've been tempted back, be it by the drugs or the money. It really has been a constant battle of wills to stay off that shit, you know. I mean, I still struggle now with it from time to time, despite how much life has changed for the better.'

Cassie resumed her agitated marching up and down the room, trying her best to avoid eye contact with her sister.

'Come on Cassie, you can't say something like that and then leave me hanging. I need to know what's going on here.'

Cassie groaned; her hands fluttered chaotically in front of her. she seemed to be struggling to decide where to take this next.

'Okay Beth, just give me a moment to gather my thoughts. We don't have very long anyway.'

Beth wasn't sure quite what she meant by that. This cryptic conversation they appeared to be having was proving to be very wearing. Particularly after the emotional exhaustion of the day. All she wanted was for her sister to get to the point of all this, so they could finish up tidying. Then she and Josh could go home and open some much-needed wine.

'Like I said, some music can affect you, who you are and become I mean. Well, I think so anyway. I think that music has the ability to spark an idea and sometimes it can be a very good one, or other times, as it turns out, it can be a very bad one.'

'God Cas, come on now, just what the hell is all this about?'

Cassie moved back to the CD player and waited. When the track on the album changed, she nodded to herself and patted the CD case before joining Beth on the sofa. Cassie took a firm holder of her sister's hands.

'Yes, this one,' she said almost to herself.

'What, this track, *Sister Morphine*? Are you actually still trying to have a fucking go at me?'

Beth tried to pull her arms free, but Cassie had a firm grip on her and she vigorously shook her head.

'No Beth. This is me, it's about me. This song, what I've done, I mean. Yeah, I was envious of you. God, I even hated you at times. But you know that, right? We have had some proper fights over the years, haven't we? But despite all of that I always loved you too, and I know you loved me, deep down. Thing is though, all I ever wanted, all ever I really wanted, was for Dad to love me, like he loved you.'

Confused by her sister's words Beth opened her mouth to protest. Cassie was quick to cut her off.

'No Beth, don't even bother. You and I both know who was his favourite. Just be honest with yourself, we both knew it was always you. Daddy's little girl. All that acting up and bad behaviour did nothing to change that, probably reinforced it, truth be told. Anyway, the truth of it is that you were the golden child and I was the one who had to grow up too quickly. I had no choice in the matter, when mum died you were so little, and I simply had to take on the role of mothering you. He needed me to be like that and for while I was happy to do it. It made me feel like I was important. Like he needed me, valued me. It also kind of helped me deal with losing Mum at such a young age, kept me busy, you know?'

Beth just nodded. She wanted to argue that her sister was wrong, that their father had loved them both equally, but there was a part of herself that had always doubted that to be true. Plus, Beth wanted Cassie to unravel this incomprehensible conversation they were having. She just wanted to understand what Cassie was trying to get to with all of this.

'But anyway, that did of course mean that I kind of missed out on being a teenager, in a lot of ways. All that young and reckless stuff largely passed me by. I feel that I didn't get the chance to become me, if you can understand that, didn't develop, mature in the same way as any other kid would.'

Beth had to admit that she had never given much thought to how life had been for Cassie when they were both growing up. She realised now that she had always viewed her sister as someone of her father's generation in a way. As a child it had totally by-passed her that Cassie was only a few years her senior. Her sister had always been that mature authoritative figure. She'd not given much thought to whether Cassie had ever actually wanted that role, or how it might have affected her.

Cassie continued, 'I think that it has all stayed with me. I mean all these years, that repressed need to act out, to be rebellious, I suppose you could call it, sort of like you were. It all got a bit muddled in my head. Then you got that job at the clinic and Dad and I thought there was such a risk of you getting sucked back into that life, you know, working with those people again, so well, I had to act. I had to do something, wanted to do something. Dad knew nothing about it of course.'

Beth felt annoyed at what appeared to be her sister's negative attitude about what she had done at the Triangle, even now. But she let the comment about 'those people' pass.

'Cas, what do you mean, had to do something? What have you done?'

'At first I just went down there. That Triangle area I mean. I, what's the term, scoped it out. Basically, I spent a bit of time watching the women down there working, saw how they did it, how you used to do it. I just wanted to understand how it had been for you, what you had gone through and what had driven you to it.'

This was becoming an increasingly uncomfortable revelation for Beth.

'Then I thought why not try? Why not me? I could do that. I could be that. The thought was so exciting, I felt like this was a revisiting of my youth, or for the first time, being the young woman that I never actually was. Being spontaneous, reckless. So, I did it. Scary at first, but I went for it, even got dressed up for it. So, it sort of didn't feel like me in the end. It was like I had an alter-ego, a braver, wilder me. I suppose. It sort of felt like a game, make believe. At first anyway.'

'Fuck, Cas. What the hell –'

'Wait, that's not it, there's more and I need to tell you it all. God, I just I don't know how you did it, Beth. Those men down there, the way they spoke to me, the way they touched me. I can still hear them, feel them. It makes me shudder. Close my eyes and I see their ugliness. I knew then that I really hated them, all of them. Hated them for what I let them do to me and I hated them for what they had done to you.'

Beth's sense of dread was growing.

'And then Dad being so ill, there was just so much medication in the house and then I found that I kept listening to this song. Over and over. I couldn't stop playing it. The words seemed to be written just for me.'

Cassie gestured towards the CD player.

'What, *Sister Morphine*?'

Cassie nodded and Beth felt like the world was slipping out from under her. It couldn't be so, could it? Cassie was acting like a mad woman. Horrifyingly it was all falling into place.

'It was you? Jesus no Cassie, it can't have been you? Tell me it wasn't. Tell me you didn't use Dad's morphine to kill those old men.'

Cassie just softly sang along, 'Please Sister Morphine turn my nightmares to dreams.'

'Oh my God Cassie, you've lost your fucking mind. Jesus, no.'

'It's okay Beth, really it's all going to be okay. They deserved it, we both know that and it was so easy. They were so desperate for me to touch them, so keen for it, that I had ample opportunity to stick the needle in. At first when I planned out what I was going to do, I thought I just wanted to hurt them. Wanted them to feel fear so that they would never return the Triangle. But then when the first one actually died, I thought this is fate. This is how it has to be. For all of them.'

'Oh God, Cas how many?'

'Oh, just the three that have been reported on. I only managed to kill those three. Dad was so sick and I needed to be at the hospital so much, that I couldn't manage any more than that.'

Beth was unsure if she was more horrified by what her sister had actually done, or by her oddly callous attitude to the acts of murder that she had committed. Where was the remorse?

Beth's head was spinning. It was all so hideous and that she had done it partly for Beth was horrifying. That in some twisted way she thought she was saving her sister. How could Cassie have done these things and now to appear to be so calm and level about it all too? It was all too much to take in.

'I've called the police,' Josh said from his position in the doorway.

He had heard it all.

214

'Josh, no.' Beth needed time to think.

'It's okay, Beth,' Cassie said firmly. 'He's right to do so. In fact, I had already rung them myself before we started tidying up. I told Peter Bloom when I saw him with that young officer that I had some information for them and that I would ring them after the wake. Sensible, grown-up old Cassie always has to do the right thing doesn't she?'

Beth could only let out an anguished howl.

'They should be here soon. It's the right thing Beth, really. I have to face up to what I've done.'

It was all happening too quickly. Beth felt she needed more time to process everything.

'Cassie I, oh God, Cas.'

'I know. It's okay, really,' Cassie said reaching a hand up to Beth's cheek.

Beth sobbed. 'No Cassie, it isn't. How can you say that it is? You can't just hand yourself in to the police like that. We need time to talk about what you have done, what is going to happen now. What we are going to do about it.'

'No Beth, the decision is made. I know what needs to be done and I'm doing it. I can't live with this any longer. It didn't take much for you to work it out, once I had given you a clue or two, so the police wouldn't have been far off either. Plus, I couldn't deal with them sniffing around thinking that it was you responsible. No, I have to face what I've done. There will be plenty of time to talk later. You will come and visit me, won't you?'

Cassie was staring at her sister, her eyes wide.

'Of course I bloody will Cas.'

The sisters embraced. Beth gripped Cassie tightly, not wanting to let her go.

'Cas no matter what's gone on or how things were between us in the past, you do know that I love you, don't you?' Beth choked.

'Of course, I do and I love you too. I only ever wanted to look out for you, wanted the best for you.'

Behind them Josh cleared his throat. 'Sorry to interrupt, but the police are here.'

Two uniformed officers stood in the threshold to the room. 'Cassie Hooper?' one officer enquired.

'That's me,' responded Cassie. She rose to stand, carefully brushing down the folds in her dress. Beth reached out desperately trying to grasp at her sister's arm. 'It's alright,' Cassie murmured and gently pulled herself free from her sister.

'You need to come with us now please, Miss Hooper,' said the same officer.

Yes of course, no problem.' Cassie left the room with the officers without looking back. Beth sunk back into the sofa cushions, a tearful mess.

Josh rushed over to her side, 'I'm so sorry this has happened, Beth. I can't imagine how you must be feeling. Oh God, Beth. This is all so awful.' Josh reached to take her into his arms.

'No, no, I need to speak to Cassie, to stop her.' Beth roughly pushed Josh away and headed for the front door.

She was too late. Cassie's was already seated in the back of the police car.

'Cassie! Let her go!' Beth yelled.

The officers in the car looked at her briefly and then turned away, adjusting their seat belts.

Cassie raised one hand. 'It's okay' she mouthed at her sister as she was driven away.

'No, it's fucking not,' Beth replied mournfully to herself. 'It's not okay, nothing is.'

CHAPTER 33

What do they call it, shell-shock? Was that an overly dramatic term for how she felt? The events of the day, of recent weeks it now became apparent, were most certainly traumatic.

Josh persuaded her that it would be best if they returned to Beth's flat. In a daze she shrugged, allowing him to lead her out to the car. The journey was conducted largely in silence. Beth was relieved. It felt oddly like she was in a horrible dream state. Cassie's revelation, how could she ever come to terms with it?

She wondered why Josh was with her. He must be a masochist to put up with the chaos of her life. He already thought she might have some sort of post-traumatic stress condition. He must doubly think so now, after the events and revelations of today.

She had given some thought to his idea about her suffering a kind of long-term stress from the trauma of the rape. Labelling it PTSD or suchlike made her queasily uncomfortable. The suggestion of it was almost embarrassing. It wasn't that she thought herself above suffering in that way, it was more that she felt unworthy of it. Odd, she recognised, but wasn't it just all part and parcel of life? Just like those horrible truths she had learnt today about what Cassie had done. Surely this was just the sort of thing that happened to someone like Beth? It was as if what had happened to her could not compete with the serious sorts of trauma others had endured.

Beth thought Josh must have worked out what had happened to her all those years ago. He was certainly smart enough to have puzzled it out. There was no way he could have known any of the details of the attack though, or the breadth of its violence, the violation, the control involved. But then no one else knew that.

Only Beth and the attackers. She had never been able to share it. Even now she struggled to call them what they really were, rapists.

Why was that?

It was just still too intense, too tender a wound for her to delve back into. Plus, there was also a part of her that blamed herself for what had happened. Stupid, she knew, but there it was. Guilt was there, no matter how logically she had tried to think about it. Had she been talking to someone else that had suffered that kind of attack, there would be no way that she would have blamed them or suggested that they were in any way at fault. So why be so hard on herself?

She might have moved her life on in some ways, but this persistent resurfacing of self-loathing was surely always going to hold her back. Reluctantly she had to admit that there was some truth in Josh's view of the matter and that she had to face this head on at some point, and it should be soon.

'I don't know why you put up with all this. With me,' Beth finally said to Josh.

They had reached Beth's street. Josh pulled the car over to park it at the first available spot. He turned in his seat, to face her. 'I love you, that's why,' he said with gentle humour. 'Also, life is never dull with you Beth,'

She managed a weak smile back. 'Come on then, let's get inside,' she said.

They entered what was an unexpectedly quiet flat. Beth sat down at the kitchen table, despondently.

'She's not here.'

'Huh?'

'Leah, she not here, she's gone, Beth. Your bedroom is in a bit of a mess. Looks like she's gone through the stuff on your dressing table. There's a pile of jewellery splayed out.'

She groaned and hunched forward, pushing her fingers into her hair. 'The only thing of value I had was one of my Mum's rings. Was there a red ring box there?'

'No, I don't think so.'

'For fuck sake. That girl.'

'I know, Beth. What can you do?'

Beth thought for a moment. The reason Leah had been here was because of her, because she had been on some kind of do-gooder crusade to save her. What a fool.

'Well, I can tell you what, I can go after her. Go find her. I'm not about to give up on her now, Josh. Not after all that's gone on, not after Cassie.'

'Do you think that's the right thing to do though, Beth? I'm worried about you, it's been one hell of a day and I think you need to rest, seriously. If Leah has gone, I think we both know it's because she'll be off scoring drugs, or making the money to do so. Maybe she doesn't even want to be helped. You can't force her, you know, and I think you need to focus on yourself right now.'

She couldn't deny it had been a terrible day and the fact that Josh was here with her meant a lot, but she couldn't just forget about the girl. It was all one big crashing mess in her head.

She had thought Cassie had softened after their father's death and it had felt like they had grown closer. She had really thought that they had started to understand each other a little bit more. Now it felt like Cassie had been a stranger all along. How could she have done those things? Then to have suggested that she had done it in some way for Beth. It was just so perverse. Too much for Beth to get her head around. With Leah leaving, Beth had a good excuse to avoid trying to make sense of what her sister had done.

'Yes, I do know all of that Josh, but the thing is I was lucky. I had Dad and Cas and they went out of their way to help me. There's plenty out there like Leah who don't have that. It's not about Leah being grateful for our help either, or that it could look to some like she is taking the piss. I just want to help her. She's young, vulnerable, whether she admits it or not, and yeah, I'm guessing she will end up back down on the beat. In fact, I won't be surprised if that is where she has headed now. If I was rattling it's where I would go. Thing is with the drugs, it not just getting over the physical addiction. It's the mental hold that's just as bad, worse really. Then there's the whole lifestyle thing. That can also have a twisted grip on you. When it's all you've come to know and it's the only way you know how to make money, then you kinda don't have too many options, do you?'

'I guess not.'

'And I'm not even that angry about her stealing from me. Yeah, it's upsetting that its Mum's ring but I know why she took it. I'm more pissed off with Carl for dragging her in to that life in the first place. He is the one who forced her into a situation where she needs to do stuff like steal.'

Yeah well, he's locked up, with no chance of bail this time. Don't worry about him Beth, he's going to well and truly get what he deserves.'

'Yeah, I know and I can't say it's not a relief that he's in custody, but how many other Carls are there out there, in the Triangle, on the beat in other towns? All treating young women in just the same selfish, callous way? It makes me sick.'

'Me too love, me too.'

She thought back to how her family had helped her get off the drugs and start the process to change her life. Sure, they hadn't always gone about it the right way. Locking her up had not been their finest hour, but at least they cared. It had been a tough process and even now after so much time had passed, she still felt that urge some days. So, she knew how it was for Leah. Someone needed to be there for her, when she was ready to make the change, however long that took, however many times she failed along the way.

'I'm going out to find her,' Beth reasserted.

Josh continued to look doubtful. 'Do you really think you're up to that right now Beth though? I mean, today has been so bloody difficult for you –'

'Yeah and today has messed my head up. I can't face dealing with the whole Cassie situation right now. No, right now it's about Leah and to be honest, I feel like I have let her down, rather than it being the other way around.'

Josh moved round to face her. 'Look, don't even start with that crap. You've nothing to feel guilty about, quite the opposite. Look, let's try to make some sense of everything.'

Beth looked at him doubtful. Didn't he understand how all of this was swirling crazily around her? You couldn't simply sort it out just like that it, it was way too complicated.

'Just bear with me Beth, I can see that at the moment everything is one big raw jumble. It's no wonder you're feeling so overwhelmed love.'

Beth grunted. 'Yeah, but it is all interlinked isn't it? I mean, where do I even start trying to unravel it all? I'm really struggling to get a grip here.'

'Well look, I think you don't need to try to tackle everything all at once. Especially not today. I mean, it was only a few hours ago that you had to say goodbye to your dad, and then there was Cassie. That's s too much for anyone to take on in one go.'

'So, when did you get so wise then?'

'I've always been a bit of a genius.'

Beth managed a twitch of the lips at Josh's weak joke. He continued, 'But seriously, Beth, let's try to sort things a little at a time. If you're adamant about doing something, then how about we decide what things you can actually alter now and what needs more time to process?'

'Okay,' Beth sighed. 'I guess we can try.'

'Right then, so what I think what we can tackle now is, first and foremost, getting Cassie a good lawyer, yeah?'

'Yes, that's most definitely a priority.'

'Well, I can help you with that, I know a couple of law firms that I can contact for you.'

'Thank you. Despite what she has done I want the best for her.'

'Of course you do. I totally get that. Then, and only then, I think you might be able to consider what you can do to help Leah again.'

'I love you; you know?'

'I know.'

They held each other tight and Beth felt more supported than she had been for a long time.

'You know that I'm still going down the Triangle after Leah though, don't you?' Beth's voice was muffled by their embrace.

'Yeah, I do. But I'm not going to let you do that alone.'

'I'm quite capable of looking after myself you know and of Leah. I can do this Josh. I don't need you to hold my hand.'

'Again yeah, I know you can and I wouldn't doubt your abilities one little bit. But there's nothing wrong with accepting a little help from time to time. I care about Leah too and I want to help.'

She hadn't thought about how Josh might feel about the matter and despite her own independent streak she recognised that having an ally, a friend, right now would be good for not only herself, but Leah too.

'Come on then,' she said. 'We'll do this, together.'

Printed in Great Britain
by Amazon